Grind Their Bones

by

Drew Cross

ISBN   1480010499

EAN   978-1480010499

'Grind Their Bones' is published by Taylor Street Publishing LLC, who can be contacted at:

http://www.taylorstreetbooks.com   **MYS**
http://ninwriters.ning.com   **Pbk**

While the story is inspired by the activities of the 'Gray Man', Albert Fish, all characters in this book are fictional, and any resemblance to anyone living or dead is accidental.

For Angela, who takes the pain away

Chapter 1

'It tastes simply divine.'

The slim, immaculately attired man raised the cut crystal wine glass to his mouth and took another small sip, smiling at the lady sitting opposite, his lips stained red by the liquid. 'Perfectly complements the food, of course. But then I'm a man of good taste, evidenced by the company I keep.'

He smiled again at his own compliment and put down the glass, beginning to loosen off his grey silk tie before he caught himself and paused.

'You don't mind, do you?'

He gestured to the tie with an open hand, looking sheepish at the momentary lapse, but there was no complaint from his companion, so he carried on and undid the top button of his crisp shirt with nimble fingers.

Overhead, the slowly setting sun cast a warming orange glow as the early evening set in, and trails of white vapour from passing planes divided the powder blue spaces between the clouds into soft-edged geometric shapes. The man ran both hands through his thick silver hair and lay back on the picnic blanket to enjoy the view up through the spreading canopy of a grand old oak. He'd chosen this spot in part for its dramatic aesthetic qualities; up here he could cook, drink, and dine surrounded by a sea of sweeping green undulations, appreciating the view with a connoisseur's eye.

It also had the added advantage of being far removed from main

5

roads and centres of population, since he hated to be disturbed when eating. From up here, the sound of a car would carry to his ears long before it came into sight, and, in the unlikely event of an approach on foot, the elevated vantage point meant that company could be avoided with ease, if he preferred.

He looked over at his dining companion, an extremely attractive, if slightly plump, young brunette with a flawless milky complexion and dazzling sea green eyes. Those pretty eyes were closed now, since she was unconscious and tightly bound in a seated position by thick ropes that ran all the way around the trunk of the vast tree. Tight tourniquets had been neatly applied around her upper arms and thighs in order to stop her quickly bleeding to death when he had expertly excised sections of her flesh with a thin-bladed knife to cook on the cast-iron skillet. The summer flies were taking an interest, but they weren't yet bothering him.

'I've greatly enjoyed your company, and now my appetite is almost sated.'

He hesitated and drank in the view of her again, trailing his eyes over her still form lit by a soft peach glow, and pausing long enough to see her fluttering chest rise and fall. He acknowledged to himself that he'd be sorry when it all had to end.

'Almost.'

The last word was a whisper, and he lifted his wine glass up to the softening daylight to see the swirling tendrils of the brunette's blood beginning to clot inside. This one had been easily the most satisfying yet.

6

Chapter 2

'So far as you can tell at this stage, did any sexual activity take place?'

Detective Chief Inspector Zara Wade addressed John Dent, the Senior CSI in charge, in a voice full of impatience. Not that it mattered to John. He had thicker skin than an elephant and he was only marginally smaller than one, towering over everybody else at the scene and working in a Zen-like state as usual.

'Impossible to say, Wade. He cut away the section that we'd have analysed and took it with him.'

He spoke in a matter of fact tone, shrugging his massive shoulders in a what's-a guy-to-do manner and carried on bagging up trace evidence. Zara knew from previous investigations that despite appearances, underneath the lumbering exterior lurked an acutely analytical brain. She also knew that trying to squeeze anything else out of the big man before he'd had time to finish processing the scene and mulling over the possibilities in his mind was like tilting at windmills, bruising and ultimately futile.

'That could be an attempt to destroy evidence of penetration, of course. Maybe we'll get lucky and find something this time.'

Aiming the statement at the tall lean figure of Detective Sergeant Lee Mead, who was scanning the horizon as if the killer might leap out at any moment.

She tried unsuccessfully to pat down an unruly blonde curl that hovered in the periphery of her vision.

7

'Perhaps he was still peckish and kept a snack for the road.'
Came the reply.

'I can't imagine that it tastes too good.'

She pulled a face, scrutinising the area surrounding the body, noting how everything about it looked staged. The killer apparently liked to calmly enjoy his meals and then took away anything that might carry a forensic trace, leaving unused replacement plates and glasses for effect.

'I wouldn't say that, ma'am.' Lee whispered softly into her ear as he passed. She felt the colour rising up in her cheeks as she remembered which part of the girl's anatomy had been removed.

She cursed herself for giving him the opportunity to flirt, and moved away to let the glow leave her face, pretending to check her phone while she regained her composure. She'd been sleeping with her quirky understudy for almost a year now, and they both knew how important it was to her career that they keep things low key. But the Grey Man murders, as the current investigation had come to be known, put them in constant maddening proximity virtually all of the time. Now they slipped up with increasing frequency.

He was looking over at her now, on the blindside of the dozen or so others who milled around, and looked inordinately pleased with himself. He was attractive all right, but definitely not her usual type. She'd always gone for older guys in the past, generally ones with dark hair, rugby player physiques and macho confidence to spare. Younger and less confident men were usually scared of her status, heading up major investigations for the Warwickshire Police. Those that weren't soon lost interest when she put in back to back eighty-hour weeks on the hunt for the latest crazy who'd gotten under her skin.

Lee Mead, by contrast, was only thirty two years old, five years younger than she was, and greyhound slim and softly spoken with it. He had the confidence part, but it was understated until he decided to let you in; on top of that he was as blond as she was, with eyes the colour of slate and a shower of freckles over the bridge of his sharp nose. His grin grew even broader as they locked eyes; he had an uncanny knack for reading her mind, and he greatly enjoyed the fact that it drove her mad.

'Ma'am!'

The shout went up from one of the more junior CSIs in John's trusted team, a youth who looked like he might need to start shaving in a couple more years. He waved her over urgently, and she swiftly obliged, dropping down into a crouch to get a better view of whatever he'd found.

'What is it?'

She caught sight of a sealed envelope wrapped in plastic.

'I think it's another letter, ma'am ... and it's addressed to you again.'

Chapter 3

'Am I supposed to be seriously bothered or not by the fact that none of our colleagues have figured it out yet? I mean, we're surrounded by Detectives all day long and flirting with each other like mad, but nobody seems to have realised that we're an item.'

Zara sighed in exasperation and unscrewed the top of a fresh bottle of Boschendal, a full-bodied South African red, pouring out two deep glasses for Hallie and me.

'Woah there girl! Easy on the pouring until we've had something to line our stomachs with.'

Hallie Bailey has been my best friend since we were in primary school. She's a smart and feisty stay at home mum now, or domestic goddess, as she's so fond of referring to herself, and I love her dearly. She invites me over for dinner at least once a week on the basis that she knows how bad my eating habits are around my hectic work schedule.

'We're still searching for the Grey Man, as he calls himself, but most of them don't seem to notice even the big details of what's going on in the world around them. This one's the scariest I've ever come across, Hals. He's supremely organised, incredibly sadistic, and he seems to genuinely relish what he does. He's not going to stop until we catch him, but how are we ever going to do that with no solid leads and no attention to detail?'

Hallie took a sip of her wine and then drizzled oil over vibrant, green asparagus before she began to cook it on the smoking griddle.

'He'll get caught because you're on the case, Webby. He might be intelligent and methodical, but he will make mistakes. They all do sooner or later, and when he does you'll be there to kick his ass and take him down.'

She smiled and tried to smooth away one of the stray curls cascading down my forehead with a hand that advertised her latest manicure. She's called me Webby since high school, when I introduced myself using my full name and was greeted with 'Wade? You mean like a duck does?' from one of our new classmates, before replying huffily, 'Yes, but without the webbed feet.' I always used to object to the nickname, but I didn't bother now since it made no difference whatsoever to Hallie anyway, and she doesn't need further encouragement to make me squirm.

'Anyway, it's just as well that your colleagues aren't more observant, or you'd both be up to your necks in hot water.'

She removed the green spears from the heat and placed them neatly on square white plates with a poached duck egg on top of each neat stack.

'I love them, but where do you even buy duck eggs around here?'

I asked, changing the subject and cutting into mine, letting the golden yolk pour out to coat the asparagus and reaching out for the pepper grinder. She slapped my hand away before it got there and wagged her finger at me exaggeratedly to tell me that it was perfect just the way that she'd served it.

'Farmers markets. You should come along sometime. You could even bring Lee and then we could all have a bite to eat. Of course he might decide to woo me for my superior cooking skills instead!'

Despite me telling her all of the juicy details about my clandestine romance, she had still yet to meet him, and now she grinned broadly.

'I can cook too, you know? I might even be better than you at it.'

I got defensive, although I'd already started to doubt my own long neglected cooking abilities. Being unable to turn down a challenge, or even just a perceived one, has long been one of my biggest flaws. I've always been unwilling to acknowledge when I need the help of others.

'I'm pretty certain you don't even know how to switch your oven on! But that settles it. You name the day, and me and Mike will bring the wine. I'm looking forward to meeting your secret toy boy lover already.'

Sometimes I was certain I should take her into interviews to interrogate suspects with me.

Chapter 4

Detective Superintendent Fred Russell projected his booming voice out into the furthest corners of the conference room, involuntarily pulling a face as he spoke, as if we could be in any doubt at all about his feelings. A low rumble of collective amusement greeted his usual non-PC delivery.

'We commissioned a psychological profile of the Grey Man from Doctor Alan Hardwick, a copy of which is in each of your hands. He has decades of experience working in secure units with some of the most infamous crazies that we've caught. Although I'm fairly certain he wouldn't express it in quite the same way. I want you all to take a few moments to digest the content, and then we'll bounce around a few ideas with regards to how we can use this to focus and redefine the hunt.'

We were gathered for a briefing session on the top floor of Warwickshire Police HQ, a pine-scented, wood-panelled room in what had once been a grand old stately home before the force acquired and renovated it in the sixties. In light of recent drastic cuts to our budget it was increasingly starting to look like we'd be searching for a new home before long though.

I scanned the details rapidly, eyes jumping back over the words again as soon as I'd finished, and my heart sinking like a lead weight. The important parts of the report rang completely counter to everything I felt I'd learned about our killer so far. A white male, forties to fifties, of average to slightly above average intelligence,

13

solitary in habits with independent financial means allowing him to devote time to victim selection. So far nothing contentious or new. Most of us accepted that guys who ate their dinner guests weren't likely to have many friends or likely to be the centre of a harmonious family unit, but after that opener it went swiftly downhill. Predominantly 'disorganised' offender despite 'staging' of scenes, history of severe mental illness resulting in contact with the mental health authorities, probable prison record for violence esp. against women, strongly driven by rage and misogynistic feelings, sexually inadequate, probably impotent, socially inept, considered 'odd' or abnormal by those around him, forensically aware. I stopped reading and tried to pull together the thoughts swarming like bees inside my head. I respected the doctor's credentials. He'd written a book a few years back on the subject of offender profiling that had been well received, after all, but this was just plain wrong.

From what we knew, the Grey Man was careful and incredibly well organised, before, during, and after the commission of his crimes. He selected victims who were anything but vulnerable; smart, successful and affluent women who would not be easily fooled, and there was nothing to suggest that they had been drugged or violently coerced into accompanying him to one of his dinner dates. I couldn't see any of them going along with an obviously mentally ill or 'odd' individual without some kind of force being necessary. If we were dealing with a violent, uncontrolled, woman-hater then surely that would be evidenced by his treatment of them before they died? By contrast, in my eyes, everything about his crimes was carefully measured, no sign of rage or violence beyond the obvious fact that he cooked them and cut pieces off them to eat. I shifted uncomfortably in my seat and tried to avoid catching Fred Russell's eye.

'DCI Wade, you're leading this investigation. What are your initial thoughts on the profile?'

Damn it, of course he was going to ask you first, especially since this guy's been writing to you. I fumbled for words that neither agreed nor disagreed with Dr Hardwick's assertions, clearing my throat several times before I began.

'Offender profiling can be a very powerful tool in narrowing the search for serial killers, as evidenced by our overseas colleagues in the US, and I for one am grateful of any help I can get right now. But however good it is, it won't catch him for us guys. We'll bring this one in when he makes a mistake, or when we pay close enough attention to spot a mistake that he's already made. In the meantime I suggest that we be mindful of the profile, but don't automatically rule out a suspect who doesn't match it until we've got other very good reasons to do so.'

Chapter 5

The Grey Man sat at the breakfast table with Lexie and Annabel taking up a knee each and scattering jammy toast crumbs all over his pristine suit trousers. He was smiling like a good granddad should and pressing down hard on the urge to wring their scrawny necks.

'Come on girls, get down off Granddad now. You're covering him in your breakfast.'

Grandma Madeleine swept the excitable tots onto the floor and showered their sticky faces with kisses, knowing how her husband preferred to be immaculate whenever possible, but the younger of the two, Lexie, trotted back over to him, grinning with bits of breakfast between her tiny white teeth and puckering up her Cupid's bow mouth.

'A beautiful young lady all smothered in strawberry jam and dusted in breadcrumbs. Delicious. I think I'll eat you all up for elevenses.'

He gave his best pantomime villain laugh and leaned down licking his lips, taking pleasure in her half-laughing, half-shrieking retreat into Grandma's arms.

'What's elevenses?'

Frowned Lexie, looking perplexed.

'It's an old-fashioned name for a snack in between breakfast and lunch.' Chimed in Grandma before he could reply.

'Anyway you can't eat people!'

Annabel joined in, running up close and aiming a gentle slap at his knee before dodging just out of reach of his mock lunge, wild blonde curls bouncing around at the movement.

'Why not? It's all meat isn't it?'

He grinned and started to move out of his chair towards them in a crouch, hands forming claws and his mouth dropping open to show off his surprisingly good teeth. The girls hid their faces in the folds of Grandmas pretty floral dress, giggling and sneaking quick peeks at him as he got closer. Strange how children of a certain age were convinced that if they closed their eyes and couldn't see you, then you in turn couldn't see them. Of course he'd seen adults revert back to that same tactic early on in his 'career' too, back before he'd managed to perfect his techniques.

'Come here!'

He scooped up a squirming girl in each arm and pulled them in pretending to bite them and then putting them back down before the action developed any substance. That wouldn't do at all now, would it?

'Delicious. A waltz of flavours across the tongue, simply divine.'

He hammed it up, smacking his lips in pretend satisfaction while the girls clapped in delight.

'What does it taste like, what does it taste like?' they chorused excitedly, hopping up and down.

'Hmmm...'

He pretended to chew and consider, winking at Grandma, who shook her head in exasperation at his antics.

'I'd say it tastes something like suckling pig. Not as good to eat as a teenager, but certainly better than a chewy old man, at least.'

That part was an outright lie. In his experience, it was the lifestyle rather than the age that gave the meat better flavour and texture. After all, if you wanted excellent beef you fed your cows the best diet possible and made sure that they exercised out in the fresh air for good muscle tone.

He bared his teeth again for them and then stopped, catching sight of the news unfolding on the television screen over the top of their heads. He paused for a long moment to drink in the details.

Another grisly find for the Warwickshire police and rampant speculation that the crazed butcher known as the Grey Man has murdered, mutilated and cannibalised yet another young victim.

Madeleine caught his interest and turned to watch too, frowning at the report and reaching for the remote control to protect the grandchildren's precious little ears from the gory details. She looked back across at him and something complex crossed her expression for a split second before it disappeared from view again and she smiled.

The look didn't bother him at all. In fact it was a good part of why he kept her around. No matter what hideous possibilities and doubts might cross her mind after all these years, and God only knew there had been revelations, she never questioned a single thing he did.

Chapter 6

It was early morning and I was out running in the woods with my mp3 blasting out 'Monkey's Gone To Heaven' by The Pixies. I was absurdly grateful for the light breeze slipping between the trees since I'd been neglecting my usual routine and living on fast food and coffee recently. But my breath was still tellingly ragged and my whole body felt like it was about to burst into flames. As I moved, I tried to avoid thinking about the case that consumed my waking moments just as surely as the monster I had to catch consumed his victims, but resistance was futile.

If man is five then the devil is six ...

Mention of the devil in the song lyrics immediately brought back the Grey Man's most recent letter, and I stopped fighting away the details to let the association stew for a while in my mind. I'd solved my very first murder case off the back of a niggling thought that had continued to crop up when I was out running, the drowning murder of an eight-year-old boy called Wayne Brown by his sixteen-year-old brother that had looked like a tragic accident, and it had taught me to listen to my instincts.

By the time I found him he was lying under the surface with his mouth and eyes open wide like a fish.

The teenager's words had caused an immediate reaction in me, an inner spark was the best I could do to describe it, as he'd spoken in a monotone that was devoid of emotion. I was experienced enough of policing in general to know that people respond to grief and loss in different ways, so his demeanour in itself wasn't necessarily unusual. It was something else that bothered me, but I couldn't put my finger on exactly what it was. When inspiration struck, it was as I negotiated a muddy footpath while out on a run, weaving from one side of the path to the other, trying to avoid stepping up to my ankles in the worst of the puddles and cursing the sudden unanticipated change from light drizzle to full-on deluge.

The puddles.

I'd stopped dead, waiting for the swirl of realisation to become more coherent, oblivious to the rain. Then it had hit me. Benjamin Brown was lying about at least one important aspect of his brother's death. I had an encyclopaedic knowledge of the facts in the case, so I knew that it had rained heavily the night before the little boy had died, and that meant that the rain water would have turned the water in the woodland pond as muddy with run-off and sediment as the puddles that I'd been dodging as I ran. He would not have been able to see Wayne's body under the surface of the water, yet he found it before anybody else knew it was there.

The realisation had been like lightning striking, and I had abandoned my run and my precious day off to go back in and re-read Ben Brown's witness statement. Sure enough it talked about the search for the missing boy, and how he had spotted his little brother by chance just beneath the surface from up on top of one of the muddy embankments surrounding the secluded hollow. The older boy had quickly started changing his story under closer questioning, with something menacing fighting to surface in his eyes at each

20

additional strand of his made up story that I pulled away, and the rest was now history.

I snapped back into the present again - past glories weren't of any use at the moment - and ran back through sections of the Grey Man's letter in my mind.

It's about possession, the desire to keep them close even though I must leave most of their physical bodies where they lie. When I hold my sacred communion with their flesh and blood we cease to be alone and apart and we become one, our molecules fusing together forever into one glorious whole.

What molecules do you suppose we share in common, Zara?

I'd committed the strange note to memory after multiple reads, and the words ran on repeat loop as I continued on my way. Were they a veiled threat or something else entirely?

Chapter 7

'So what do you think about Doctor Hardwick's analysis, Wade?'

Detective Supt Fred Russell always looked like he'd trapped his dick in his zipper, even on a good day, although there was an unproven rumour circulating that he'd once almost smiled back in the eighties after solving a long-running and difficult to crack serial rape case.

Today was not a good day, and there was an even more livid red than usual creeping into his round face; today he was preparing a press release designed to appeal to those who might know our elusive killer, and it was on the doctor's instructions. Russell looked like he'd been presented with a shit sandwich and then asked to eat it with great relish for public viewing. Looking at his complexion and bulging waistband, I started to fear for his heart.

'If I can speak frankly, sir?' He impatiently nodded his assent. 'I think it's peculiar, to say the least. Some of it runs completely against all of the instincts of our best detectives, guys and girls who've been working the case for months and months, and the bits that don't are those that anybody with even a small amount of common sense could have established for themselves. I think it's potentially hugely damaging to the direction of our investigation, and I don't think we should be relying on it at all.'

I knew without him saying that he was having the same thoughts, albeit he'd have expressed them considerably more bluntly, and we both knew he would personally take on the lion's share of the blame

22

if our fears were found to be well placed after we went public with this.

'I want you to hold the fort while I play politician for the papers, and I want you to be quiet about the fact that we're going to pay little more than lip service to the good doctor's profile. He's been right when officers have been wrong in the past, and he wasn't shy about pointing that out. He's something of a media darling these days, so we could do without looking like chimps if we're missing something that he spotted. Anyway as far as I'm concerned, we assign somebody junior to looking into the mental health angle, particularly since we've already been there, and we keep focussing on the few quality leads we do have while we pray for a breakthrough.'

He stopped talking and rubbed at the bump on the bridge of his nose with thumb and forefinger, looking suddenly much older than his sixty years. I found myself wondering how far away retirement was for him, not that I was so grasping that I had designs on his job, but all the same I wouldn't say no when they came and asked.

'Understood, sir.' I groped around for something else to say that might make him feel better. 'I think he feels some kind of connection with me, sir. I don't know what the nature of that is, or why he feels that way, but by writing that letter he was giving me something else to go on. That was his first big mistake, and it was a deliberate one. If he's starting to take chances, then we're heading towards the home straight.'

I mentally kicked myself as soon as I'd finished the sentence, why do I always have to try too hard to please? The truth was that we'd not even figured out which route we were on yet, the home straight was nowhere in sight.

'I hope so, Wade, I sincerely do.' He straightened the knot of his tie and turned to walk away before stopping in his tracks. 'Catch this sicko for me and the fact that you're screwing young Mead, or anybody else that takes your fancy for that matter, won't have any bearing on your career progression at all. Not that it bothers me anyway, he seems like a nice enough kid. I'll catch you later, Detective.'

He didn't look at me as he spoke, so I was spared the indignity of him watching my face take on the same hue as his own.

Chapter 8

Dr Alan Hardwick, star forensic psychologist and regular consultant over the years for several different police forces in respect of serial offenders, kicked off his new shoes and rested both feet on his grand mahogany desk. He had a generous measure of a particularly fine cognac in the balloon glass that he swirled in his chubby left hand, and the scent of the rising vapours tickled pleasantly at his nostrils. It smelled of success. With the police going public tonight with the psychological details of the suspect they were pursuing, he could start to relax a little more. His plan was coming together beautifully.

He checked his expensive watch, a Breitling Navitimer, impatiently, willing the press release forwards. It was his sincere hope and belief that the broadcast of a profile so utterly removed from the reality of the man they were seeking would give the killer a green flag to up his kill rate significantly. After all, if the police and their best profiler couldn't come up with an accurate new direction for the enquiry, and in the utter absence of any other real evidence of note, why wouldn't the so called Grey Man grow in confidence? Come on, let loose and feed the beast like you know that you want to.

Hardwick knew this one was beginning to escalate already anyway, two in as many months, taking his tally up to seven that they officially knew about so far. The doctor could be certain he'd found more hiding in among the frightening number of unsolved cases, but he wasn't going to be sharing that little nugget of knowledge with his occasional employers just yet. Not with so much money at stake.

He sighed and signed into his personal computer with one hand, taking a mouth full of the brandy and holding it in his mouth to let the complex flavours develop. He was certainly no connoisseur, but he thought he could detect the vanilla and honey undertones the tasting notes had mentioned lingering on his tongue when he eventually swallowed. There'd be time and money to develop a connoisseurs palate once this was all over, let there be no doubt about that.

The screen whirred to life and he deftly navigated over to a file entitled 'accounts', double clicking the icon and scanning down the numerous sub folders that opened up below. It took him a couple of seconds to relocate the one that he wanted, but that was perhaps unsurprising in view of the number of glasses of the cognac that he'd treated himself too since he'd arrived home. Hell, he deserved them after months spent studying, obsessing and worrying, it was almost time to start the celebrations, just a simple matter of waiting.

He didn't really need to read the contents any more, he'd spent hundreds of hours of his own time reading, researching, speculating and refining the short coded document already. He'd obsessed over all of the finer details, and even revisited case notes from his time interviewing half a dozen high profile serial killers in prisons and secure institutions up and down the country. However, he took comfort in the reassurance that revisiting the Grey Man's profile gave him, and he took further comfort in the sheer amount of planning and craft that went into the string of horrific crimes. Of course, the profile was very, very different from the one that the Warwickshire detectives were currently scratching their heads over.

He strongly felt that this one could be the best of the worst, killing for years to come without making the mistake that would catch him, until he completely eclipsed the score that other UK serial murderers had managed before they found themselves dead or behind bars. There was a good chance that he'd already managed that feat, but this would make that certain, and then the headlines would resonate around the world. They needed to in fact, he was counting on it.

Hardwick himself would control what that tally would be and how long that spree would last, the recent letter had seen to that. You see Doctor Alan Hardwick had done the unthinkable for a profiler; through expertise and careful analysis, with just a tiny bit of pure dumb luck thrown in too, he'd worked out exactly who the killer was for himself.

Chapter 9

'We believe that we're closer than ever before to apprehending the serial murderer known as the Grey Man, and we've taken the operational decision to release certain aspects of his likely physical and psychological profile, prepared by no less than the country's foremost forensic psychologist, to allow members of the public at large to assist us in bringing this hunt to a swift end.'

Fred Russell looked vaguely ill under the strong studio lighting, and the gathered throng of photographers and reporters seized on that small sign of possible weakness like a pack of wolves, competing to take the best shot of the glistening beads of moisture on the senior officer's brow for tomorrow's front pages.

'The man we are seeking is older than your standard fit for these types of crimes, in his fifties or even sixties, but still retaining sufficient physical strength to restrain and keep captive healthy adult women. It is the doctor's strong assertion that this man has come to the attention of friends, family and colleagues as behaving in an odd or abnormal fashion, and that his rage towards women in general has manifested itself in the past, resulting in incarceration and likely contact with the mental health authorities. Contrary to some of the speculation in the media, we believe that he is of no more than average intelligence.'

He stopped to tug at his tie distractedly, and took a long gulp from the glass of water sitting alongside the row of microphones in front of him before he carried on.

'He isn't going to be wearing a sign advertising the fact that he likes to kill and eat people in his spare time. But there are those of you out there who know this man and who suspect there is something deeply wrong about his demeanour, particularly around the times that he's committed these appalling offences. I would urge you to raise your concerns through our dedicated switchboard, so we can narrow the number of names on our suspects list down to the one individual who is responsible for holding us all to ransom. Don't be concerned about reporting somebody who you have doubts about, but who you may not feel is capable of such atrocities. We'll very quickly be able to clear those who are not of interest to our enquiries. Thank you.'

He stepped back away from the plinth and obvious relief flooded back into his features. He was careful to keep his face turned away from the camera flashes so they wouldn't catch the displeasure creeping back in.

Detective Russell, what would you say to those who feel this is little more than hollow posturing – an empty gesture designed to try to flush out a killer who is always two steps ahead of the police?

Is it true you once called psychological profiling 'mumbo-jumbo crap made up by head-shrinkers to justify their hourly rate'?

Fred, if he's not especially smart then why have there been no breakthroughs despite at least seven women having lost their lives?

If he's in his fifties or sixties, what earlier cases are you considering as being the work of the same man? Don't they typically start out in their twenties and thirties?

29

He pushed his way through them like the bulldozer of a man he was, palming aside the expensive cameras that were thrust towards his face and trying to keep as cool as he possibly could. Fucking vultures.

When he kills the next one, and you're still no closer to catching him, what are you going to say to that girls parents?

The last question hit a raw nerve and he spun angrily back around, scattering those closest to him with an outstretched arm.

'Which one of you parasites asked that last question?'

He looked around not expecting a response, reporters weren't renowned for their physical courage.

'I did.'

The man who stepped forward was barely out of nappies, a skinny runt with bad skin and teeth, wearing an off the peg tweed jacket that belonged on a much older person. He looked inordinately pleased with himself, and several of the other reporters took pictures of him as he moved out into plain view, sensing a storm brewing.

'If we don't catch him before that happens then I'll tell them exactly what I'm telling you now. That while scum like you are rubbing their hands over the amount of money you can make out of their daughters suffering, I'll be busting my balls until my dying day if it takes that long to make sure that this monster pays for what he's done.'

Chapter 10

It was just after eight in the evening and I was feeling pretty relaxed for the first time in a long while, enjoying an ice-cold cobra beer with Lee in an intimate little Indian restaurant called Kismet on Leamington high street. The smells of cinnamon, coriander and chilli permeated the air around us, and the gentle buzz of casual conversation punctuated by occasional laughter was pleasantly soothing and hypnotic.

'You're grinning like a Cheshire cat, Wade.'

Lee stroked my leg with intent, his bold actions hidden by the chequered red and white plastic tablecloth.

'I'm happy to be here with you, Mead, especially since you're springing for the bill.'

I chuckled and took another refreshing sip of my lager, watching his eyes twinkle and dimples forming in his cheeks when he returned my grin.

The waiter arrived in a cloud of exotic scented steam before Lee could think up a smart reply, depositing the house special Akhbari Lamb on the table between us with a flourish as more staff arrived with half a dozen brightly coloured side dishes and arranged them all around us. I inhaled deeply, trying to separate out cardamom, ginger and fenugreek, and feeling my mouth start to water copiously.

'I take it we're switching our phones off for a change tonight, since we're enjoying each other's company so much?'

We had been disturbed on almost every other dinner date that we'd been on, and it had become a kind of running joke between us. Murderers and psychopaths don't take nights off just so detectives can live some semblance of a life outside of work. We both knew that we'd be leaving our mobiles on discreet just in case there was either an unexpected breakthrough or another murder in the Grey Man case. We both wanted to catch him before another young life was cut horrifically short, and being disturbed over dinner or in bed was a small price to pay for the knowledge that another maniac was off the streets.

'May I?'

Lee gestured towards the lamb, and I nodded enthusiastically and watched him start to serve up for me. It never ceases to surprise and delight me that behind the smart-arse façade lurks one of the last true gentlemen.

'I love this place, Lee, it's like this guy I know from work, straightforward and non-showy on first glance, but with hidden surprises underneath.'

I forked a mouthful of succulent spiced lamb and pilau rice into my mouth and started to chew with a cheeky wink.

'You left out the hot and tasty parts too, and, like the food, I'm guaranteed to make you sweat.'

He offered me a wink of his own in return and spooned chilli pickle onto a crisp poppadum for himself.

'So what did you think of Russell's performance?'

He asked, referring to the farcical press release.

'I think he looked like we all felt. Uncomfortable and unhappy with the details we've just been asked to release, but all in all he held it together pretty well. I'm still trying to get my head around how Hardwick's got this so apparently wrong though. His credentials are impeccable, and his previous psych evaluations have been spookily accurate. Did you know that the gutter press ran an article on him half a dozen years back after he helped out in a big case and he sued them over it?'

He shook his head and I carried on.

'They compared him to the people he was helping to catch. Implied that it takes one to know one and dug up all kinds of dirt from his past.'

I paused and sampled the Bombay potatoes, moist, fragrant and with a subtle kick on the aftertaste, easily the best I've tasted outside of Birmingham's famed Balti triangle.

'Great food and no disturbances so far, wonders will never cease. We might even manage dessert at this rate.'

I raised an eyebrow holding his gaze with unconcealed intent, purposefully moving the conversation away from work, as a slow knowing smile crept across his face.

'Detective Inspector, I want you to know that I will be only too happy to fully fulfil all of my duties with due care and diligence.'

I took another swallow of beer before I replied.

'That's pleasing to hear, of course. Although as the senior officer here, there's still an awful lot that I need to teach you. It's likely to be a long, hard, night.'

Chapter 11

The phone rang at seven thirty and dragged me back to a state of reluctant consciousness. I felt heavy limbed and still half-saturated with lager and red wine from the previous nights festivities with Lee, and my head had developed a heartbeat all of its own. I could hear Lee singing in the shower, and my puerile mind quickly made a quip about early risers. He never seemed to suffer the way that I did after a night of over indulgence, but then again he was still only a baby at side of me, I reflected bitterly.

'Damn it!'

I stumbled clumsily into the bedroom doorframe and bashed my shoulder hard enough to bring tears to the corners of my eyes, but at least it woke me up enough to slide unsteadily down the stairs, clutching onto the banister for support.

'I'm coming, I'm coming for Christ's sake!'

I shouted at the insistent ringing from the hallway.

'What?'

I answered the phone aggressively, forgoing my usual pleasantries in annoyance. My number was ex-directory and registered with the Telephone Preference Service, so it couldn't be a random sales call. Who the hell rang at seven thirty on a Sunday anyway?

'Wow! Nice to speak to you too big sis. Didn't wake you up did I?'

My baby sister Emily's voice emanated from the receiver and my heart sank.

'Whatever gave you that impression? After all it's practically the middle of the day.'

I knew as I spoke that the sarcasm would be wasted on her, she's as immune to it as she is to insults.

'Good. I've been up since six with the kids as usual, no rest for the wicked. Have you been drinking, you sound kind of slurry?'

I sighed deeply, rubbing at my temple with my free hand and silently praying for her to emigrate some time very soon.

'No, I had a stroke when I heard your voice coming down my phone. Have you called for anything in particular, or just out of concern about my drinking habits?'

Lee emerged from the bathroom and started to come down the stairs with a cream coloured bath towel wrapped around his waist. He caught me admiring his toned torso as he passed, and promptly whipped the towel away to give me a view of his bare backside, prompting my first grin of the day in spite of how I was feeling.

'David's gone and left me again. Can I come and stay with you for a few days?'

She spoke matter of factly, this would be the third time that her cheating rat of a husband had walked away and we were all starting to get used to the cycle. Even Mum and Dad had started to come round to my viewpoint and had recently started telling Emily that she was better off without him. I couldn't understand what she'd seen in him in the first place. He was habitually arrogant, aloof and cold towards virtually everybody around him, and I'd made no secret of the fact that I didn't like him on the few occasions when we'd been

35

forced to spend time together. His family were little better, with his father expecting his poor downtrodden mother to run around after them all like a good little wifey. But then I guess some people seem happier that way.

'What about the children? I don't exactly have acres of space around here, as you know.'

I wondered why she hadn't gone to our parents place like last time, but after their change of heart about David I thought that might be at least part of the answer.

'They're staying with David's parents for the time being while we both get away for a few days to think about our future. So can I stay? You know I wouldn't ask if I wasn't desperate.'

I heard the coffee maker coming to the boil through in the kitchen and I wobbled before finally caving in.

'Okay, but just for a few days. I'm in the middle of a big murder enquiry and I don't have time to sit in and deal with your problems for you.'

I put the receiver back down so I wouldn't have to listen to her gratitude and wandered through to pour myself an industrial sized mug of coffee and to break the news to Lee.

Why am I such a bloody push over?

Chapter 12

The Grey Man pushed his foot down a touch harder on the accelerator and the new silver Jaguar XKR surged forward in response. He was usually as careful with his driving as he was with all other aspects of his life. It didn't pay to draw attention to yourself unnecessarily when your main hobby was the killing and eating other people. But he was a significant distance from civilisation on a single track country lane, so the risk of being caught speeding was a small one.

The plan had been to scope out possible suitable settings for his next little soiree, but there had been disturbing developments in the police investigation that were playing on his mind. Now he found himself, for once, largely ignoring the vivid expanse of varying greens blurring past the windows on either side.

The biggest problem lay in the press release, which he'd awaited with growing excitement and anticipation. This would be the time when the famed Doctor Alan Hardwick entered the fray and gave an eerily accurate description of the Grey Man for all to hear. Then the games could really begin. On the evening of the scheduled broadcast he'd booked himself into a boutique hotel for the evening, making excuses about an unplanned business trip to Madeleine, and packing a modest overnight bag. She had accepted his explanation without question or complaint, of course. His sudden absences were frequent enough that they no longer raised any eyebrows and he'd been free to lay his mask to one side for a while.

'His rage towards women in general has manifested itself in the past, resulting in incarceration and likely contact with the mental health authorities. Contrary to some of the speculation in the media, we believe that he is of no more than average intelligence.'

The words had bounced around inside the dark recesses of his mind until he finally skewered them in place and began to carefully dissect them. Was it possible that the great Doctor Hardwick had him down as a garden variety lunatic? A deranged, dribbling, uncontrolled sadist lashing out at any woman who crossed his path, and who existed in police records for his prior offences?

He'd obtained copies of each of Hardwick's previous books, even taking the trouble to get them personally signed, feeling immortal as he'd watched one of the world's foremost authorities on serial killers look him in the face from a mere three feet away on two separate occasions, and still not see him for what he was. He'd pawed over them for hours, marvelling at the powers of deductive reasoning that had undone some of the greats and brought their bloody sprees to an end. He was a worthier adversary than the rest of them put together, perhaps the most dangerous one who had ever lived. How dare the man disrespect him in this manner?

The Grey Man snapped back into the present, brushing away the cobwebs of remembrance and slowing the car back down again at the sight of a flock of young sheep crossing the road a hundred yards ahead. The flat-capped shepherd raised a hand in acknowledgement as he came to a complete halt, and he fiddled with the radio channels to kill time while the animals clambered all over each other to get through a break in the dry stone wall. It was a well worn cliché, but people were indeed like sheep, they lived in a state of constant neuroticism, and the whole lot of them could be scattered in panic by the presence of just one predator in their midst.

The more he considered it, the more unlikely it seemed that the esteemed Alan Hardwick could have gotten his evaluation so obviously wrong. They were beginning to forget how much they should fear him, and that meant it was time to scatter the flock again. It was time to pay the Doctor a visit.

Chapter 13

Unable to shake off my grave concerns about the psychological profile of the Grey Man that Doctor Hardwick had provided, I had made an appointment to meet with him at his home office in the Coventry countryside near Ryton on Dunsmore. The surrounding greenery on the short drive out, with golden sunlight streaming across rolling open fields, made a welcome change from my usual airless windowless surroundings lit only by flickering fluorescent strip lights, but soon had me reaching for my sunglasses. Evidently I'd have to start finding more reasons to get away from my desk before I started growing fangs and anaemia set in.

His home was practically an estate, with electronic gated access that necessitated me climbing out of my car and announcing my presence, before I was permitted to drive along the winding gravelled driveway. The house itself told me I should have concentrated harder at school, being as it was, a grand example of what bespoke architecture and a bottomless wallet can achieve together. I brought the car to a gentle standstill and stepped out, dropping my sunglasses on the driver's seat, and taking in the view of floor to ceiling glass held in place by a network of thick oak beams.

The front door was already opening before I'd even completed my appraisal, and the Doctor's wife, a tiny pale smiling lady with a waist so improbably small that I thought I could get two hands to meet around it if I wished, bounded energetically into view.

'Good morning, you must be Zara.'

I locked the car, immediately wondering why I was bothering in such surroundings, there was infinitely more likelihood of it being broken into on my own doorstep than here.

'Yes, guilty as charged, Mrs Hardwick.'

I jogged up half a dozen gleaming wooden steps to greet her, offering my outstretched hand.

'Please call me Anne, Mrs Hardwick makes me feel every single year of my age.'

She ignored my hand and instead opted to pull me into an unexpectedly tight hug, forcing me to stoop to accommodate her and enveloping me in a cloud of floral perfume tinged with something chemical that I couldn't place.

'Well thank you for making me feel so welcome here already, Anne. From the outside your home is really quite something. I'm starting to feel guilty for bothering your husband on what is probably a fool's errand.'

I delicately extricated myself from her insistent grasp and put some space between us, and noticed for the first time how glassy her stare was, as if she was intoxicated despite the hour.

'Oh the Doctor won't mind. He's big on investigators following up their hunches, he's even started research on it to try to isolate what that intangible factor is that experienced detectives seem to have which points them in the right direction time and time again. Yes, the house is rather lovely, we had it built to our own specifications in fact, it's just a shame that we'll be moving out soon.'

I barely had time to process the strange formality in how she'd referred to her husband, when her face suddenly dropped and panic bloomed in her eyes.

'Oh my! Here's me keeping you standing on the doorstep waiting when he's expecting you.'

She grabbed hold of my hand and practically pulled me into the house, shutting the door behind us with a bang. Then started to usher me quickly through the hallway, with its galleried staircase, and towards the rear of the property.

'The Doctor has an office down at the end of this inner hallway here.'

She stopped at the head of the passageway and pointed, clearly expecting me to continue onwards alone.

'Thank you, Anne. Can I just ask why you're planning on moving home? I mean, if I had a place as beautiful as this I can't imagine ever wanting to leave.'

The question hung in the air for a long moment before a deeper voice answered on Anne's behalf.

'That's what I like to see, a detective who can't break the investigative habit, even with their colleagues. With your successful track record I sincerely hope I'm not on your list of suspects, Ms Wade?'

Chapter 14

I felt my face working up to a scarlet glow as I sheepishly turned round to meet Alan Hardwick. I'd been caught in the act of crossing a line by digging into his private life and we both knew it.

'I am so sorry Doctor Hardwick, it was force of habit, and a bad habit at that. Shall we retire to your office so I can grovel?'

He didn't seem to be overly concerned by my questioning of Anne and laughed at my response.

'There's really no need, Detective Chief Inspector, I know you meant no harm by it. Follow me this way if you please?'

The Doctor made a sweeping motion with his chubby arm and waited for me to fall in step beside him, I noticed that he was four or five inches shorter than my five foot ten and that he had a purplish coloured birthmark shaped like South America in the middle of the expanding bald spot on top of his head. He stayed silent until we entered his study.

'Please have a seat and tell me what it is that's bothering you?'

He shut the door and manoeuvred himself into a leather, high-backed, swivel chair that was raised up high enough to allow him to look down on me.

'Coffee?'

He gestured towards a shining, silver, Gaggia coffee machine perched on his desk and I nodded enthusiastically.

'Yes please. As for why I'm here, I alluded to it on the phone, but I'd rather be completely blunt if that's okay with you?'

I watched him as he carefully organised my drink, placing the cup on a fancy looking saucer to catch any spills. He's fastidious to a fault, not at all like the kind of person to put out a report that he wasn't entirely happy with.

'I get enough evasiveness from my charges during the course of a normal working day, if indeed you can call any day in Forensic Psychology entirely normal. Be as blunt as you like Detective.'

He smiled displaying slightly stained and crooked front teeth, which were at odds with the rest of his immaculate presentation.

'Okay. I disagree with your psych evaluation of the offender that we're calling the Grey Man. It doesn't concur with the modest amount of other evidence that we've obtained so far, and it seems to run counter to the theories and models that you espouse in your own books.'

I added cream and sugar to my cup and stirred quickly before taking a sip and making eye contact with him.

'Thank you for your honesty at least, but I'd have to counter that assertion by asking you where exactly you obtained your doctorate in the subtleties of behavioural science?'

There was a definite edge in his tone and I sought to clarify my position.

'My qualifications are of the variety that you can only obtain by catching a number of serial offenders for yourself.'

I'd intended to continue but he cut me off before I could do so.

'Perhaps you've decided that there's some sinister hidden agenda here, and that despite a long and illustrious career helping your

44

colleagues up and down the land to solve the unsolvable and catch those responsible for the unthinkable, I'm deliberately misleading the investigation? Or better still, you've been reading the latest crime novel and decided that I'm the Grey Man. Is that it?'

His voice had risen dramatically in volume and he was now visibly in a rage. I stood up to leave, aware that my welcome had been well and truly outstayed and trying unsuccessfully to keep my own quick temper under wraps.

'Your wife assured me that you'd have no problem in assisting a police officer who was following up on their hunch, Doctor Hardwick, and it was not my intention to insult or demean. But I have to say that your behaviour gives me pause for thought. Just why exactly are you selling your house?'

I opened the door and stood my ground, fixing him with a level stare.

'Show yourself out before you cross another line with me, woman. I'll be speaking to Fred Russell before you're off the driveway and you'll be directing traffic by morning.'

Chapter 15

'I don't know what it is yet, but there's something wrong with Hardwick, and I'm going to find out exactly what that is.'

I stuffed home-made basil and sundried tomato pesto mixed with cubes of tangy feta into the cavity of a plump chicken breast with more force than was strictly necessary, while Lee took care of the salad.

'Hey there Blondie, don't take it out on dinner or we'll prove Hallie right about your lack of cooking prowess.'

He rinsed his hands under the tap and dried them on a tea towel before wrapping his arms around my waist and resting his head over my shoulder to watch me work. He'd saved the day by remembering the dinner party that I was supposed to be throwing for my best friend and her husband tonight, and had turned up with bags of food and alcohol and a set of favourite recipes for us to construct together. If I hadn't been so pissed at the dressing down that had greeted me when I'd arrived back at headquarters following my meeting with the Doctor, then I'd have been overwhelmed with gratitude.

'Russell didn't even have the good grace to do it privately, so now everybody knows that I screwed up.'

I pulled an exaggeratedly unhappy face and he kissed me on the cheek, smoothing back stray tendrils of my hair.

'Here, let me take over with this and you can have a glass of wine while you watch.'

He let go of me and retrieved a bottle of Argentinian Malbec from one of the bags, pouring me a half glass and then rolling up his sleeves to deal with the rest of dinner.

'You should have taken me with you today, you know?'

He slit an incision in a fresh piece of chicken and widened it out with his finger, expertly forming a pocket for more of the fragrant filling. His voice was soft and impassive, but he has a habit of pointedly not looking at you while he talks when he's emotional about something, and he was using the task to hide that fact. I'd been so consumed by my dissatisfaction that I'd gone to run my errand without even thinking about asking him to back me up; now he was hurt.

'I'm sorry. I guess I didn't want to drag you into something that was just based on a niggling doubt. I didn't think for a minute that it was going to go anywhere and I was right.'

I took a mouthful of the wine and let it wash around my mouth before I swallowed it, watching his lack of reaction and trying hard to read his mind.

'You've been around me long enough to know that I don't make any unnecessary demands of you, Zara. Even though I sometimes might want to.'

He looked up and smiled at me with a hint of sadness in his baby blue eyes.

'But I'm going to make a demand of you right now. I need you to promise me that you'll include me at all levels of this investigation. That means mundane door to door crap, crazy hunches and wild goose chases too. We might not yet know much about this one, but from what we do know, he feels enough of an affinity for you to take the time to find out your name and write to you. That gives me a very bad feeling about the whole thing.'

He finished up the last of the preparation and placed the chicken onto a foil lined baking tray sliding it into the hot oven. I opened my mouth to continue the conversation but the doorbell disturbed us. Mike and Hallie had arrived, I could see her dark hair through the opaque glass.

'I promise.'

I said and went to let them in.

Chapter 16

The evening was proving to be the perfect antidote to my day. Mike and Lee had hit it off right away and were already loudly conspiring about golf weekends and football matches while gesticulating with their bottles of Budweiser, and me and Hallie were already well into our second bottle of red wine and giggling like school girls over everything and nothing.

'So I'm taking it that this delicious dinner wasn't entirely your doing, Webby?'

Hallie was grinning and looking decidedly inebriated. She'd been dieting hard for the past three months and looked great tonight in a fitted red dress with matching, chunky, costume jewellery bangles. Earlier in the evening she'd surprised me by asking if she could join me on my evening run a couple of nights a week, making me promise to take it easy on her to begin with, and I'd enthusiastically agreed to the idea.

'The recipes were all Lee's doing, but I did stuff the chicken breasts.'

Lee stopped talking and raised an eyebrow at us across the table.

'Okay, okay! I stuffed one and a half of the chicken breasts before he took them off me for being ham-fisted! I did turn the oven on unaided though!'

We all laughed and Mike raised his glass.

'I propose a toast to agreeing to do this more often.'

We brought bottles and glasses together with a clink and drank our approval to the suggestion.

'So, are you going to make an honest woman of her any time soon, Lee?'

Hallie was trying to look innocent, but mischief sparkled in her dark brown eyes as she dodged away from the good-natured slap that I aimed at her bare arm.

'Hals! Leave the poor guy alone, we've only just taken this first step towards going public and you're already booking the reception!'

I felt Lee's eyes resting on me and I beamed at him to let him know that I wasn't appalled by the idea, feeling heat rising in my cheeks.

'I think Zara's easily the most wonderful woman that I've ever met. I can't imagine wanting to have anybody else in my life. Once we've ironed out her reckless streak of course!'

They all laughed together and I made a show of giving them a mock scowl before relenting and joining in.

'I'll take that answer for now,' Hallie replied and shared a knowing look with her husband.

'Moving swiftly on. Who'd like dessert?'

I stood up and started to collect in the empty plates, with Lee following suit.

'It's okay, I'll get these. You can stay and entertain for a minute while I plate up,' he said, reaching out to take them from me.

'Definitely a keeper.'

Chimed in Hallie, loudly enough for him to hear as he headed for the kitchen, starting to giggle and taking another sip of wine to hide her amusement. Mike put his arm around her shoulders and leaned in to kiss her gently on the neck.

I'd watched him playing with their twin boys for hours on end in the back garden at summer barbeques, and admired how natural he was around children. I liked children a lot, but had somehow never seemed to manage to make time in my life for anything besides the job until Lee came along. Now I knew that the clock was well and truly ticking for me if I ever wanted to be able to chase children of my own around without the use of a frame.

Lee appeared to applause from our guests, carrying plated up individual chocolate mousses topped with cape gooseberries.

'They look wonderful, I can see I'm going to have to up my game for the return match at our place.'

I knew that was high praise indeed coming from Hallie. Any doubt that had ever existed about whether she would approve of my choice of partner was now well and truly gone.

A persistent knocking at the front door disturbed me before I could try a spoonful, and I waved Lee back down into his seat and went to answer it, glancing up at the clock to see that it was after eleven at night. Who the hell turns up for an unannounced visit at this time of the day?

I opened the door to see my sister Emily leaning heavily against the porch wall; she was clutching a half empty bottle of vodka in her hand and black tears streaked down her cheeks where her eyeliner had run.

'You're not supposed to arrive until tomorrow.'

Was the best I could manage, stepping aside to let her in.

'I thought I'd surprise you...surprise!'

She slurred, and then started to cry.

Chapter 17

'She's the human equivalent of a black hole. Everything that's around her gets sucked into her problems time and time again.'

I lay on Lee's chest in bed, with Emily passed out and snoring fit to raise the dead in my guest bedroom at the opposite side of the landing. I was absolutely furious with her for disrupting our perfect evening, but at least Mike and Hallie had been incredibly gracious about the intrusion. They'd stayed for long enough to finish desserts and a digestif before deciding to walk back to their own home half a mile or so away, and left us to the unenviable task of sorting out my staggeringly drunk baby sister.

'I don't know that much about the history between you, other than the little that you've told me tonight, but she's obviously going through a rough time at the moment. Don't you think you might be being a bit hard on her?'

He ran his fingers through my unruly curls, straightening them out and letting them spring back again.

'Believe me when I say that I've gone above and beyond the call of duty in letting her stay at all. We all warned her about David when he first arrived on the scene. He's all charm and smarm on the surface, but look beyond that and there's pure selfish egotism running right the way through to the other side.'

I kept my voice down, even though there was next to no chance of us waking up sleeping beauty.

'It's not a crime to be selfish and arrogant. There are plenty of people who would level the same accusations at me if they were asked.'

I hesitated before I replied, questioning the wisdom of sharing the next part for a split second before I spoke.

'There's more. But you'll have to promise to keep it to yourself after I tell you.'

I manoeuvred myself around so my chin was resting on the pillow beside him and I was looking into his eyes, which appeared to be as dark as my own in the absence of light.

'You have my word.'

I couldn't read his expression, but he sounded interested.

'Last time they fell out, Emily turned up at my parents with bruises on the tops of her arms, which she said were just from being clumsy, and they rang me immediately. I decided to confront him first instead of talking to her about it and tracked him down to his parents place.'

I paused to collect my thoughts, feeling the tension creeping into Lee's arm as he caressed my side.

'Anyway, I read him the riot act on domestic violence, told him that I'd kick his arse from there to the cells if I was ever even given cause to suspect that it had happened again, and that I'd be telling my sister to bin him along with the rest of the trash.'

I stopped again, thinking about the weird expression that had crossed his face.

'Did he try to deny it?'

Lee asked, looking wide awake now and moving into a sitting position.

'He didn't say anything at all. Just stood there with such a spaced out look in his eyes that I wondered whether he was on drugs, and then his father came over and spoke on his behalf instead.'

I yawned, feeling my anger beginning to dissipate and the fog of sleep beginning to descend on me.

'What did he say?'

Lee was impatient for me to finish.

'He just said, that would be a mistake Zara, in his most business like voice and ushered me right back out of the door like I was the hired help. My talk seemed to do the trick though, none of us have seen a scratch on her since, and until now they've seemed as good as they've ever been together. I presume he told her about my visit though, because she's not had anything to do with me since. Now lie right back down here Mister, I was comfortable where I was before.'

He did as he was told and slid back in beside me, mulling over what I'd just said.

'Yet you're still the first person she's reached out to this time, and that should tell you something.'

I reached around and started to stroke his inner thigh in response, slowly working my way upwards.

'So should this.'

I whispered, moving my hand inside the waistband of his boxer shorts.

Chapter 18

Under the cover of darkness the Grey Man slipped over the top of the modest garden wall and dropped quietly to the ground. For all of the show of security features at the front of the property, with gated electronic access and closed circuit television cameras, the security round the back was shockingly poor; a pleasant ten minute walk across open fields from a quiet country lane and he was standing within view of the property. Evidently the Doctor had no real fear of meeting those who might wish him harm here at his country retreat, although to be fair to him, obtaining the address hadn't been as straight forward as anticipated.

The ground was hard underfoot, courtesy of the glorious summer that they were having, and an evening that had been entirely free from moisture of any discernable kind; so it appeared that the precautions he'd taken with footwear would prove to be unnecessary. He didn't trouble himself to stay down low or move at speed across the open spaces, since he'd already taken the trouble to disable the motion sensor on a floodlight that kept watch over the neatly striped lawn on a previous recent visit. Besides that, the Doctor was a man of almost neurotic routine and habit, retiring to his bed full of expensive brandy at ten every night almost without fail. He'd be asleep and snoring next to his lunatic wife by now.

The Grey Man was a man of considerable means. He continued to hold a position as a Director on the board of a successful company that he had founded some years ago, simply in order to provide cover for his comings and goings, rather than out of strict monetary necessity. With that money and power he'd been able to discreetly find out a considerable amount about Doctor Alan Hardwick. Certainly a lot more than the good Doctor would know about him, even if his suspicions on that score were proven correct tonight. One of the surprises had been the wife, Anne. It had transpired that she was a former patient of his, who had been exonerated from culpability in the death of her abusive ex-husband on the grounds of diminished responsibility. That fact appeared to have escaped the notice of almost everybody, but then again, she had changed her name by deed poll after her eventual recovery and release from a secure unit. The psychiatric evaluation prior to release had been done by Hardwick himself.

Upon reaching the back of the house, he was greeted by the sight of several open windows, an additional benefit of the muggy summer nights that made pastimes such as house-breaking that much easier. He quickly slipped inside, removing the bag from his back to ease his passage through the opening, and headed for the spectacularly beamed master bedroom.

It seemed curiously lighter inside than out, courtesy of all that glass combined with the light and airy décor, which made navigating the unfamiliar territory more straightforward. Knowing the floor plans of a property was not quite the same as physically being in it, but the layout was a testament to beautifully designed natural and logical flow. In any other circumstances that might well be a good thing for Doctor and Mrs Hardwick. He pushed open the door to the master suite and stepped inside switching on the light. Nobody was there. How was this possible?

'I knew you'd come after the floodlight was tampered with the other night, so I've taken to sending Anne away as a precaution in the evenings.'

Doctor Hardwick's voice came from the darkened study behind him, and the doctor himself switched on the desk lamp as he spoke and came into view.

'I must say that I'm so very pleased to finally make the acquaintance of the feared Grey Man. Perhaps even more so because I was right about your identity.'

Alan Hardwick's face was alight with excitement. He looked like a child standing in front of the world's largest pile of presents on Christmas morning.

'Now don't go getting any ideas about killing me too. I've got your real psychological profile on my computer, together with your real identity and the chain of logic that allowed me to work out who you were. There's a hardcopy lodged with my solicitor to be opened immediately in the event of my death, since I was almost certain that your reaction to the insultingly bad press release would be to track me down. It's been a nervy couple of days of waiting, since you disabled the light outside, let me assure you! Of course, I had to make sure I was awake to tell you these things, otherwise… well, I hardly need to tell you about that now, do I?'

Chapter 19

The Grey Man moved into the study space without outward signs of surprise or concern; taking the time to examine the framed certificates covering one wall.

'Very impressive, Doctor.'

He said without feeling, placing his bag down on the desk top and slowly clapping his hands together in an approximation of applause, watching the smaller man fighting the urge to flinch back into his chair.

'And what, may I ask, was the clincher for you?'

He maintained eye contact for longer than necessary, enjoying Hardwick's growing discomfort and watching beads of sweat breaking out on his bulbous shiny head.

'I'd already been working on the theory that you felt you had a connection with the lead Detective, you'd alluded to it obliquely in some of your previous correspondence. A shame that the investigators assumed that it was only a connection that you felt you shared, and not one that existed for real. I, on the other hand, had a strong feeling that it went some way beyond that. I followed my nose and the circumstantial evidence until you came onto my radar, and then my suspicion was confirmed. It's quite astonishing when you think about it. Not to mention on many levels somewhat pleasing, and all the more incredible when you consider that you are there in the police records for all to see, questioned but never charged in relation to a seemingly unrelated but nevertheless very important incident all that time ago. The most recent letter that you left was what confirmed it once and for all for me.'

Hardwick stopped talking and gave a small shy smile. Was it possible that the man was star struck?

'Very astute of you, Doctor. And now we stand here, two men with a common interest I believe. So just exactly what do you want from me?'

He began to undo the clips on the backpack, reaching inside to remove the contents and starting to place them on the top of the desk.

'I want the opportunity to gain an insight into you, to establish the details of who you are, what forces shaped your earlier life, and what you do when you're alone with your victims, as well as getting your take on why that is.'

He paused for a moment and then delivered the punch line.

'I want to be the first man in my field to conduct a detailed examination of an active serial killer who is still at large, and in return I will keep my findings entirely to myself until such time as you are incarcerated or die. Regrettably, they are statistically speaking very likely to catch you at some point, even without my help. Although I'll ensure that I am of no use whatsoever to their investigation in the meantime.'

The small man smiled again, looking immensely pleased with himself.

'And what use are those findings to you at that point, Doctor?'

The killer finished removing the last of the items from his bag.

'They'll be going into my book about you of course. Along with details of the revised psychological report that I prepared after the first version, which was almost completely accurate, and which was roundly ignored by my police colleagues who chose instead to consider me as a potential susp...err...what are you doing?'

Hardwick's sentence tailed off as he noticed the length of rope in the other mans hands.

'Showing you my equipment, Doctor; the tools of my trade if you will. If you want to understand what I do, then it's important for you to see this next part for yourself.'

He formed a loop with the rope and fashioned a slipknot before deftly swinging it over the seated Doctor and pulling it tight in one practiced fluid movement.

'I'm not sure that this is entirely necessary...'

The incapacitated man started to protest feebly, growing increasingly concerned. The intruder ignored him.

'I was privileged to visit Morocco last year, a beautiful place full of all manner of curious delights, particularly of the culinary kind, and for that reason it's a place that features high on any true gourmand's wish list. Have you been?'

He looped the rope around the back of the chair several times, pulling it tight enough to constrict Hardwick's breathing.

'Not yet. That's a bit tight by the way.'

The captive man's face was already beginning to change colour.

'You should have done. They have one delicacy that's not for the squeamish, but which is surprisingly good if you're prepared to take the plunge. It involves feasting on a whole roasted sheep, something which they do socially and communally. Do you know which parts they consider to be the best?'

He paused to allow the Doctor opportunity to reply.

'Remember about that envelope lodged with my solicitor.'

Panic started to fill Hardwick's expression and he struggled feebly against his bonds as he spoke with a rising pitched voice.

'The eyes and tongue, Doctor...which are considered to be so good that they are sometimes eaten fresh and raw.'

Chapter 20

It was technically my day off, so I'd been looking forward to spending some time kicking back and relaxing at home. But I didn't trust myself to hold my tongue around Emily, so I showered and dressed early before heading out into the irritatingly cheerful morning to catch breakfast away from the house. Lee rose with me, stopping to ask whether we should really be leaving her to wake up to an empty house, and prompting me to leave a terse note explaining our absence, along with a spare key in case she decided to head out for some air too.

'So where are we heading?'

I was moving at a fast march, putting distance between myself and my sister, something that I'd been trying to do continuously without much success since childhood, and Lee was looking bemused by my haste.

It wasn't that I hated her, after all she'd never done anything deliberately designed to hurt me, but she'd had an unfortunate knack of attracting trouble for as long as I could remember, and I preferred a less complicated existence. I knew I couldn't express that sentiment to Lee without sounding cold and unkind, but life was always that bit more difficult with Emily and her host of problems around, circling like sharks on the periphery. I'd met many people like her over my years in the police force, and it was never their fault, but ultimately they always ended up as another one of life's born victims.

'I need coffee so strong you could stand a spoon up in it and something disgustingly sweet and pastry based for breakfast. Any suggestions?'

I turned my head to look at him and he mimicked my scowl, lightening my mood instantly.

'There, that's better. You could pass for thirties again now!'

He dodged the punch that I aimed at his arm.

'I vote for the Pump Rooms. They'll just about be opening up by the time we get there, although at the speed you're moving I could always hop on your back and you could sprint down the motorway to London instead if you prefer!'

He laughed and earned another begrudging smile from me in return.

'Pump Rooms it is then, but I reserve the right to bitch about my sister when we get there, whether you like it or not, okay?'

He nodded his assent and we fell into easy silence for the rest of the stroll, moving along scarcely populated streets and admiring the predominantly Georgian buildings. I didn't bother to slow my pace, trying to punish him for laughing at my expense, and we covered the mile and a half to the handsome Royal Pump Rooms, responsible for Leamington's 'Spa town' tag, in a little less than half an hour.

Once seated inside I headed for a window seat in view of a flat screen television up on the wall that was playing the local news, while Lee went to sort out our breakfast order of coffee and assorted pastries. The volume was down low so I couldn't quite catch what was being said, but I recognised the background behind the stern faced reporter as being Rugby town centre, since I'd spent many days and nights on foot patrol there when I was back in uniform.

'Excuse me...'

I waited impatiently for the smiling young girl serving Lee to acknowledge my presence, but it took her a moment to finish fluttering her eyelashes at him for long enough to register my voice.

'Could you turn this up please, there's something I want to hear for a minute.'

She nodded and produced a remote control from under the counter, turning it up just enough for me to catch the detail of the report.

'Local people are baffled as to why this particular building, home to the solicitors firm Johns Gilbert and Frankton, was targeted, but the firebomb almost completely destroyed the premises before fire-fighters were able to get it back under control.'

Lee wandered back over with a plate of croissants, Belgian buns and chocolate twists, looking up at the screen to see what had piqued my interest.

'The coffees are coming over in a minute. What's up?'

He set the plate down in front of me and helped himself to a croissant.

'Can you think of any earthly reason why somebody would want to destroy a solicitor's office?'

I eyed up one of the Belgian buns and then changed my mind and went for a chocolate twist.

'Lord knows I've wanted to every time they get some little scumbag off the hook to continue leaving a trail of destruction. But, no, it's not something you see everyday, I suppose.'

We didn't get chance to continue the conversation, as both of our phones began to ring in unison.

Chapter 21

The scene in Doctor Hardwick's office was horrifying.

Thick clots of gore had been smeared across the impressive bank of certificates on his wall and a fine spray of blood seemed to coat every available surface. I could almost taste it in the air. The windows had been left open all around the vast house, and fat summer flies danced a lazy bloated waltz around what was left of the Doctors face. I fought hard not to look at it again, but found that I was unable to keep my eyes off his corpse for more than a few moments at a time, and eventually opted to leave the room to compare notes with the crime scene investigators.

'Any initial thoughts?'

I walked up to the giant form of John Dent, who was filling out labels for items of potential evidential value that he'd seized.

'Well, don't quote me on it yet, but I'd say that he's definitely dead.'

He grinned, showing off teeth the size and general colour of tombstones.

'Why do you think he took out the eyes and tongue?'

I tried again, hoping for some spark of an idea that might tell me what the doctor's death was all about.

'If you wanted to be literal about it, it could be punishment for something he'd seen and then talked about, perhaps. Then again, he came into contact with a lot of crazies, so it could just be that they had a fixation and decided to keep those parts as trophies. You tell me, you're the Detective, I'm just here to clean up.'

Dent looked thoughtful as he replied. Many people find him caustic and difficult at times, but I didn't think there was any real malice behind the words, just statement of fact.

'Thanks John, believe it or not I think you just helped.'

I smiled at his furrowing brow.

'I assure you it was completely unintentional, Wade, so don't go spreading that around, I've got a rep to maintain.'

We were disturbed by the sound of footsteps approaching. Lee holding a plastic wallet with an envelope inside. The neat lettering on the front was immediately familiar.

'It was him.'

He didn't need to elaborate on who he was talking about, but I mentally struggled to reconcile the carnage in the office with the controlled and staged scenes that we'd grown accustomed to at the Grey Man's previous murders.

'If it was then this was entirely different for him. There was nothing in there that looked controlled to me this time.'

I thought about the pulp that now constituted a face, with empty hollows as eyes and a tongueless mouth stretched wide open, frozen into an agonised final scream. Yes he was a vicious psychopathic sadist, he excised chunks of flesh from still living victims and then cooked and ate it in front of them, but everything that we'd seen before was done in an altogether more orderly fashion. This was a different kind of butchery, not simply about excising the tasty parts. The Doctor pissed him off.

68

'That answers the question about where the other bits of his face went anyway. If we can come up with something clever to explain what happened this time round then we'll stand an infinitely better chance of catching him. Anybody got any ideas?'

Lee looked thoughtful as he spoke, looking in my general direction but straight through me at the same time.

'The most obvious one is that he didn't like the psych profile. Perhaps it was too close to the truth for comfort and he started to view the Doctor as a threat?'

John Dent offered over the top of his considerable shoulder, as he stuck the last of his labels on a container and then walked away.

'Maybe, but after my chat with Hardwick I'd put my pension on it that he was hiding something, and that profile was just all wrong on every level. I guess it could be that the killer was offended by the press release, most psychopaths have egos the size of small planets, and they don't need excuses to add to their tally.'

I felt that needling feeling that signalled the start of a connection again, but it remained maddeningly just out of reach.

'He had a computer in his office when I visited, did you see anybody seize it?'

I didn't see any of the tech guys at the scene, and with John Dent presiding over things, CSI wouldn't just grab it without making us aware of that. Lee shook his head and frowned.

'JOHN, JOHN?'

I shouted at the back of Dent who was exiting through the front door and he turned back around. The niggling feeling was growing much stronger now. Whatever had prompted this visit had been on Hardwick's computer.

Chapter 22

The turmoil after the discovery of Alan Hardwick's body, and the scrabble for meaning after my subsequent realisation that the Grey Man had taken his personal computer, made me all but forget about my sister's presence in my house. Lee took the cowards way out and made his excuses at the end of a frustrating extended shift, and left me to return home to deal with her alone. It was starting to get dark as I quietly opened the door and let myself in, so I expected her to be tucked up in bed, at least I hoped she would be. So it would be an understatement to say that I was surprised when she greeted me in the hallway with a glass of wine and ushered me along to the neatly set dining table.

'I didn't know when you'd be home, and I didn't want to bother you at work by calling to ask, so I've gone for things that are quite simple to do.'

She fussed around in a flurry of activity before disappearing back into the kitchen. I was already beginning to feel guilty about my blistering appraisal of her to Lee earlier, when she re-emerged with elegantly presented starters on my best plates, and the guilt deepened.

'It's pan-seared loin of tuna with a mustard and dill crust on a salad of mixed baby leaves and herbs. The main course is a mixed seafood linguini, you really are spoiled for choice with fresh ingredients around here.'

Momentarily speechless I took a mouthful of the fish and started to chew. It was absolutely delicious.

'When did you learn to cook like this? It's superb, by the way, thank you.'

I avoided meeting her eyes, trying hard to hang on to my resentment towards her uninvited intrusion into my world, and not wanting to watch her smile with pleasure at the first complement I'd given her in recent memory.

'David adores fine food and drink, he's practically obsessive about it, and my initial efforts when we first got together weren't entirely palatable! So I took classes over the internet while he was away on business, followed by a few hands on night classes at a local catering college, and now I'm starting to get pretty good.'

I glanced up as she mentioned his name, trying to gauge her general mood after the previous night's histrionics. She looked despondent, but mercifully the tears stayed well away this time. Ironically, for somebody in my chosen profession, I've never been much good at comforting distressed people. I prefer to catch the animals who cause the distress in the first place, and then see to it that they pay for their actions with years of their lives spent in a lonely cell.

'Well you should be proud of yourself, Emily, this is as good as I've eaten in any swanky restaurant.' I forced a smile this time and looked across at her. 'I definitely didn't get the cooking gene from Mum, I could burn water, but thankfully Lee's more in your league in that respect so I don't starve. Do you want to talk about what's going on at home?'

I took another forkful of tender tuna and herbs to hide my discomfort as the silence started to stretch out.

'No, not just yet, if that's okay? I'm happy being here for a break and getting away from it all for a few days for now. Not that I'm planning on treating you like an hotelier.' She took a quick sip of her wine and glanced at me before continuing. 'Thank you for this, for letting me stay, I mean. I couldn't face any more questions from Mum and Dad right now, and I knew you wouldn't pry like they do, not with everything that you've got going on.'

I raised my own glass in acknowledgement, smiling again to let her know she was welcome. The deep red liquid looked like blood in the dim light, and I thought of the monster in human form still out there who apparently toasted his dinner companions in much this same way, and I silently promised them that I'd catch him no matter what.

Chapter 23

The Grey Man letters were never opened and read at the scenes. They were always sealed in ordinary everyday envelopes of the variety that could be purchased in any high street stationers, and so far they had all been utterly devoid of anything that could be of evidential value in identifying the killer, beyond the obvious fact that they were handwritten. However, there was always that small chance that he'd slip up, so the forensics team conducted their examinations of the documents before they were released to me. I'd tried to hard to find ways to keep myself occupied while I awaited receipt of the latest one, but patience is not one of my virtues, and I was slowly driving Lee mad with a string of unanswerable questions about the case.

'What are the possible motives for him killing Doctor Hardwick?'

I was pretty much just thinking aloud, but Lee sighed deeply and stopped what he was doing, turning his chair away from the computer to answer me.

'Well, we now know how much debt the doctor had managed to amass, so there could be a motive in there somewhere, but it seems highly unlikely. The smart money's got to be on the profile and the press release pissing our psycho off, and prompting a visit either because it was too close to the truth, or because it was deemed to be offensive by the killer somehow.'

He massaged two days worth of stubble with his thumb and forefinger and looked past me into the distance.

'So we're agreed that the key to this one's in that profile somewhere?'

I waited for him to nod his assent and then carried on.

'And we're both agreed that the profile's got to be wrong...?'

He nodded again, more impatiently now.

'It's completely out of leftfield Zara, especially for a guy who's been so accurate on almost every other notable occasion. What are you driving at, exactly?'

He started to look interested despite his apparent frustration.

'What if it was deliberately wrong?'

We locked stares and I paused to let the suggestion sink in.

'I want us to discreetly do our own profile of the Grey Man, one that ignores the speculation as far as possible and focuses on what the evidence tells us.'

I stopped again to check that he was still onside.

'Okay. And what exactly is that going to achieve?'

He frowned, but at least it wasn't outright resistance.

'I'm not one hundred percent sure just yet, beyond clearing out the crap and clarifying what we genuinely know. But it does give us a good reason to access any records that the good Doctor himself had a look at recently, don't you think?'

We shared a slow knowing smile.

'You think there's something else in there that might have been held back?'

I watched Lee entertaining the possibility as he spoke, seeing the first glimmer of anticipation sparking in his eyes as I nodded my head.

It made some kind of sense that Hardwick hadn't shared everything that he'd found out, otherwise why else would the killer have taken his laptop? Maybe he'd given us an inferior profile to work on while he worked on another angle, after all, he could always have let us in further down the line when he was sure about his facts without looking bad. There'd have been grumbling, but in the press it would be another famous victory and that was surely worth big book sales for his next opus.

We knew now from speaking to his wife that there were significant gambling debts in the background, and that they had been looking at selling their home just to survive. Perhaps he was gambling on a bigger hand, perhaps he'd even thought that he could catch the killer before we did? I'd seen it time and time again. Desperate people are driven to desperate acts. I felt the stirrings of my inner crime solver nodding along in approval.

Chapter 24

Grandma Madeleine discreetly watched her husband brooding while busying herself preparing the girl's dinner, he looked uncharacteristically haggard and drawn, and she knew that spelled trouble if she wasn't careful. He'd hardly spoken a word since arriving home this morning with the smell of petrol and smoke in his hair, casually handing over his clothes for washing without explanation. She'd flipped on the television in the kitchen and scanned the news stories, until the local broadcasts came on.

A famous forensic psychologist had been found brutally murdered at his home and the police were being tight-lipped about the details for now, and elsewhere in the county somebody had firebombed the empty offices of a solicitors firm for reasons as yet unknown, recounted the breathless young reporter. She breathed an inward sigh of relief at the second piece of news and took some small comfort in the aroma of his hair, then looked around for the remote and put it all out of her mind. If she chose to ignore it then it hadn't really happened at all.

'You should take a shower while I make lunch, I'm serving sea bass.'

She studiously avoided his gaze as she spoke, keeping her tone even and conversational, not a trace of accusation creeping in. He'd not vented his inner rage on her in several decades, but when he was like this, with demons swimming behind his dark expression, she was extra careful not to push the wrong buttons anyway.

'I'll do that,' he eventually replied, turning his head to watch the girls running around on the decking in the growing warmth of the sun. The light caught their tanned arms and legs, which had been liberally coated with factor fifty sun cream before they'd been allowed out, and they glistened like basted poussins, mesmerising him for a long uncomfortable moment before he drained the last dregs of his strong coffee and retreated to the bathroom.

Madeleine watched him go with real concern. He usually tried to engage with the girls in his own fashion, which she knew wasn't easy for him in view of his own upbringing. This morning he hadn't bothered with them at all. She went across to the open French doors and leaned out to let the girls know that lunch would be ready in five minutes, and stopped to watch them play, taking genuine pleasure in their spirited haphazard waltz.

'I'll eat you all up!'

Shouted the youngest girl, making a grabbing gesture at her fleeing sister and baring her perfect white baby teeth.

'No, I'll eat you all up now!'

The slightly bigger girl suddenly switched roles and whirled back around, catching her laughing breathless sibling by the wrists and tumbling onto the warm dry grass with her, giggling fit to burst.

'Your lunch will be on the table in five minutes girls; that's if you've got enough room left for it when you're done eating each other all up?' she enquired, still smiling benevolently. The girls looked at each other and laughed some more, before the eldest assumed position as spokesperson.

'We're being a greedy Granddad who eats little girls.'

'Just like a giant!' Chimed in the other one and giggled.

'Okay, well I'm off to start putting lunch onto plates in a moment, remember to wash your hands when you come back inside please.'

Her smile remained fixed in place, but an adult would have noticed that it took more effort now. She was thinking about the dead girl again, as she often did when her husband's behaviour took a turn for the worse. She wished for the thousandth time that she'd never played any part in making the girl disappear forever.

Chapter 25

Do the people who believe they know us best really know us at all? How well do we even know ourselves until we take the time to explore those hidden recesses that house our darkest desires? These are some of the questions that trouble my waking moments, and I wonder whether they trouble other members of my species in the same way, but I strongly suspect not.

Doctor Alan Hardwick believed that he knew me from a hand full of snapshots of a single facet of who I am, and from that he believed that he could predict my actions when we finally came to meet. Yet with all of his years spent dissecting his fellow human beings, when push came to shove he was still wrong.

I took his eyes and tongue because they were wasted on him, Zara. What do you suppose that you could live without?

I stopped reading the Grey Man's latest note and jotted down my immediate impressions, aiming to capture my gut reaction before my deeply ingrained need to analyse everything took over. Lee was away slowly working his way through the details of Hardwick's comings and goings over the last six months, looking for anything that might help our unofficial composite profile. I wrote down three words in auto-pilot before I had to stop and re-read what had come out. They were simply: WE HAVE MET in thick black capital letters, not exactly the depth I'd been looking for. I tried to dig underneath the thought, to expose the roots of where the notion had come from, and I leafed back through transcripts from the other seven cases to try to pinpoint exactly what it was.

Do you still retain the ability to feel for them Zara? If it's true that repeated exposure to horror blunts the human emotional response as a coping mechanism, then we're not really so very different after all. I wasn't always a monster.

I've never known what it was like to be entirely 'normal', and in a different way you too turned your back on normality to pursue your chosen path in life, Zara. Did they tell you how much it would cost you when you started out? Nobody was there to tell me how every single small step was another step away from the rest of the human race either.

It's almost funny to contemplate now, but the first time out I was physically sick with fear. I lived in agony for the longest time afterwards. The second one was better. They seemed to be playing a role, and I have to say they were perfect in it. Don't you find in life that some people are born victims, Zara?

I stopped reading and looked at my three words again. Not 'have we met', but 'we have met', a statement not a question. This man had made me part of his fixation, which was not a new consideration, it had already been raised a dozen times throughout the ongoing investigation. The problem was that we'd never been able to nail down why that was. A review of some of my old cases had been held in an attempt to identify whether there were any viable suspects from my past, who might type as a possible Grey Man, but there'd been no breakthrough and we'd dropped it in favour of other potentially more productive avenues of enquiry.

I'd been a murder detective for eight years now, but I'd been in the force for fifteen, and there'd been interactions with too many criminals of all varieties to hope to be able to quickly recollect one in isolation who might be capable of offences like this series. Truth be told, I'd met a hundred who struck me as capable of serial murder and mutilation, violent angry men with holes where their hearts should have been. All that most of them lacked was that additional unknown factor that might transfer their rage onto strangers as objects to act as an outlet for their warped reasoning, rather than those poor unfortunates who chose to live their lives around these human time bombs.

I sat back and tapped the pen against the top of the desk, contemplating my options and ticking them off in my mind. I needed to approach this case differently. This man had reason to feel a connection to me, and I was certain that we'd met, even if it had been more significant for him than for me. I needed to make a list of every man I could remember coming into contact with throughout my career so far, not just the obvious lunatics, if he'd been one of those then chances were we'd have found him already. I needed to begin methodically ruling them out one by one until the last man remained.

Chapter 26

Eleven thirty at night and I was throwing my best shapes on the crowded dance floor in a trendy club with Emily. It was incredibly hot among the tangle of lithe sweating young bodies, and the fact that I found the music both too loud and completely unfamiliar should have been proof enough that I was too old for this stuff now. This impromptu night out had been another one of Lee's bright ideas, and he's waved me and my protestations away from work with a laugh, a lingering kiss, and a cheery 'have fun, but not too much'. Surprisingly, my sister hadn't needed asking more than once when I brought up the possibility of a night on the tiles, and now we were both pleasantly drunk on over-priced cocktails. Anybody watching would never have guessed that there had been any animosity between us to begin with.

A group of testosterone oozing students were starting to move in our direction, so I decided to beat a tactical retreat, gesturing to Emily that I was fit to drop, sticking out my tongue and crossing my eyes to emphasise the point and noticing again how alike we looked when she laughed. I knew she wouldn't be able to hear me properly until we got away from the giant speakers, but I trusted that she would follow me out into the fresh air and I began to apologise my way back to the doors.

The drop in temperature back out on the street was exaggerated by contrast with the oppressive humidity inside the club. I immediately began to shiver as the moisture on my skin suddenly cooled and my clothes starting to press up against me uncomfortably. I looked up at one of the largest moons I'd ever seen hanging in the night sky, breathing in big lungs full of the crisp air and wondering why it looked so close sometimes and so far away at others.

The seconds slipped past and Emily still didn't emerge to join me, I pushed aside my annoyance and fidgeted impatiently, plaiting my hands together for warmth and checking the messages on my phone to pass time. Lee had sent me a smiley face and a single kiss an hour ago, but for once the rest of the world was allowing me to have the night off.

'Where the hell are you, sis?'

My breath formed the suggestion of a cloud as I muttered to myself and rubbed at my bare arms in a feeble attempt to restore some warmth to them.

'Fuck this.'

Mind made up, I went back inside and starting retracing my route back to our spot on the dance floor in case she'd missed the point and decided to stay put.

I was greeted by a sauna-like wave of heat and the rhythmic bass thump-thump of a track that sounded exactly like the last dozen or so that I'd heard since we'd arrived. Two tanned and shirtless young guys with matching short Mohawks moved into my field of vision, treating me to pelvic thrusts presumably designed to impress me, as I was forced to squeeze in between them to pass. I looked from side to side intently, scanning the sea of unfamiliar faces as I moved, but

Emily was nowhere to be seen. I wasn't quite tall enough to see as far as the bar, but I decided that I'd head for where we'd been first before doubling back that way if she wasn't there.

I fought hard to keep the rising sense of unease inside me in check, but I could feel the tension forming knots in my back and neck as I started to lose my cool. She wasn't dancing and after skirting back around I couldn't see her in the crowd at the bar either. I checked my phone again, nothing, and horrible considerations began jostling for attention in my head.

Chapter 27

I hesitated and weighed up the options, eventually deciding to check out the ladies loo's before I started causing a scene. Perhaps she'd had more to drink than I'd realised, and was washing her fringe in the toilet bowl right now. There was quite a queue developing when I arrived, so I was forced to loudly explain myself half a dozen times as I negotiated my way towards the front to look inside for Emily, and even then I had to endure a sea of hostile stares.

'Emily ...? Are you in here, Sis?'

My voice echoed back off the tiled walls, but there was no response. Unsure what else to do I pushed on the nearest one of the cubicle doors and it swung open to reveal a rough looking redhead snorting a line off the top of the cistern.

'Do you fucking mind?'

She scowled and kicked the door back shut in my face. Count yourself damn lucky that I'm otherwise engaged, missy, or I'd have you in the cells tonight for that.

I took a deep breath and moved on to the other two with no luck on either, then gave it up as a bad job and decided to head back out towards the door staff I'd seen lurking in the lobby.

As a general rule I try to avoid prejudging the diverse range of people that I meet, having long since learned that they have a tendency to spring all manner of surprises on you when you're least expecting it. However, as I approached the group of bouncers for help, all of whom had no necks and shoulders that appeared to sprout from out of their ears, watching them nudge each other and snigger, I doubted somehow that they were discussing the finer points of neuroscience and astrophysics, and my guard shot straight up.

'Hi, my sister Emily was in here with me and now she seems to have disappeared from view, I was wondering...'

Before I could finish what I was saying the head doorman cut in.

'She probably went home, or to somebody else's home, but I could always keep you company now if you're left all alone?'

He leaned his arm across behind me in a move that could be interpreted as either protective or as preventing my retreat, and my inbuilt moron detector virtually exploded.

I pulled out my warrant card and thrust it up into his face, holding it there for long enough for him to register that I was no mere beat bobby, and catching him wilt slightly as he took his arm back out of my way.

'That's better. as I was saying, she looks like me, but brunette with shoulder length straight hair and wearing a tight red dress. I'm sure you'd have noticed her, since you'd have had to retrieve your piggy little eyes from her cleavage when she passed.'

I smiled sweetly and without sincerity, watching him exchange a worried look with two of the other gorillas.

'What?'

I asked impatiently, waiting to be let in on what they knew.

'She headed into the gents about five minutes ago with a group of guys.'

His expression burned with dawning realisation at the whole world of shit he was about to land in, and he suddenly found it hard to meet my stare.

'Just so we're clear. You watched an obviously drunk woman being led into the male toilets by a group of guys, and you didn't do anything about that? Say goodbye to your licences gentlemen, if that term can be applied to low lives like you.'

His eyes suddenly flicked up and past me, and I tensed as I felt a hand rest on my shoulder, relaxing again when I heard a familiar voice.

'It's okay Zara, I'm fine, I just want to go home now,' said Emily, and then threw up all over my shoes.

Chapter 28

'Just when I was beginning to believe that we were making progress, she went and screwed it all up royally again.'

I was over at Lee's ultra neat rented house mouthing off about Emily and her antics again, noticing how this was rapidly becoming a feature of my life at the moment. Lee was fresh faced and chipper this morning, in stark contrast to my current condition, and his evident enjoyment of that fact was doing nothing to help my mood. I was nursing the kind of hangover that made anything more strenuous than blinking painful, and I was pretty sure that I looked like the bride of Frankenstein right now.

'Not that I necessarily approve of what she did, but it's not exactly a hanging offence in this day and age, and she's hardly the first person to seek a little solace in strangers, is she?'

He took a gulp of coffee and reached for a slice of buttered toast, smiling as my stomach performed a spin cycle and I glared at him belligerently.

'For the record, if you ever find yourself seeking solace in the arms of a stranger then make sure that you really, really enjoy yourself. Because, by the time I'm through with you, it'll be the last time that you're physically able to perform that particular act.'

I could feel the heat of indignation rising up in my face.

'Don't worry, in that department I'm more than happy with my lot.'

He flashed me another boyish grin and took a big bite out of his toast.

'What am I going to do with her, Lee? She's in her early thirties now, a wife and a mother, and she's out behaving like a teenager. I thought she'd been assaulted to begin with, you know? Then when we got outside and she finally started to make sense, it turned out that she'd been quite happy to oblige a group of strange men like some streetwalker, and that it's apparently not the first time she's felt and acted on that particular urge.'

I sighed in frustration and chewed at the ragged corner of a fingernail, pushing my unruly hair back with my spare hand.

'And that's her choice, Za, so don't take responsibility for that on your own shoulders.'

He put down what was left of his toast and moved around the table to hold me, enveloping me in the sweet smelling scent of a new Issey Miyake aftershave that I'd bought for him.

'She'll be just fine in the end, you'll see. She just needs this time to find herself before she'll be ready to be a mum and resume all of the related responsibilities again. All you can do in the meantime is listen when she wants you to and bite your tongue until she asks for your opinion.'

He played with a loop of my hair as he spoke and I almost forgot about my hangover.

'You're probably right as usual, but it's not going to be easy to keep my mouth shut about her recklessness last night.'

I closed my eyes as a heartbeat took up residence in the centre of my forehead, pulsing at double the rate of the steady rhythm in Lee's chest. I tried to blank out the pain, but it felt absurdly like I was being

90

punished for the fact that I was keeping some details of the previous night back for now. I wanted to mull them over some more before I invited anybody else in.

Does he suspect what you've been doing? I'd asked, referring to Emily's husband, David. Good God, no! He'd kill me if he did know...actually murder me. It's in him somewhere, I've seen it in his eyes sometimes. She'd said, and then passed out, leaving me alone with my thoughts in the darkness.

Chapter 29

The girl was absolutely perfect in every possible way. A study in blossoming grace and femininity, with long wavy chestnut coloured hair and bright blue eyes that might have been piercing if it wasn't for the warmth that radiated from her expression. The Grey Man would have taken her for one of his private dinners a long time ago given the chance, but there was one crucial detail that had made that an impossibility in the past. The girl worked for him, and as such knew who he was and had seen the face that he chose to wear like a mask for the world that existed outside of his fantasies and desires. He had always been careful to ensure that there were no clear links between his real self and his victims. Well, almost always his inner voice corrected. You nearly learned that lesson the hard way very early on in your career, didn't you?

He watched her through his office window, able to observe her bathed in glorious morning sunlight without her being able to see him in return due to the angle of the blinds, but she glanced up at the glass from time to time anyway, as if a sixth sense had alerted her to his scrutiny, and each time she did she smiled shyly before resuming her work.

He'd already done some research into her life, unable to completely let go of his desire to own her, so he knew that she was single and living with her widowed mother, who was suffering with the onset of dementia or some other similar ghastly ailment. The absence of a boyfriend seemed to be a consequence of her duties in caring for mum, giving her very few opportunities to mix with her work colleagues or friends outside of the office. That kind of isolation tipped the balance back in favour of dinner slightly.

He gave up on work and shut down his laptop, running his gaze back over her for the twentieth time, drinking in the details of her curves and noticing how there was only one other worker in the large open-plan space with her at the moment. Eventually, his frustrated scrutiny gave way to his desire, and he decided to see whether the scenario in his mind might play out after all. It wasn't like the police were getting close to catching him yet anyway.

She looked up from her desk as the door to his room clicked open and he emerged, and she smiled demurely with the ghost of a blush drifting up into her cheeks as he made pointed eye contact with her. He knew that even though he was old enough to be the girl's grandfather, she was attracted to him on some level, and why not? He remained in impeccable physical condition, having retained good habits from his time served in the navy all those years ago, and he was very affluent. The years had been kind to him, making him look more distinguished than weathered, and he had excellent manners and a good natured welcome for each and every one of his employees when their paths crossed. In his line of work it paid to be an exceptional actor, and he was one of the best, living out the vast majority of his time playing this role, with only the one or two people closest to him having ever glimpsed one of his other faces.

'Good morning Elizabeth, in bright and early as usual I see.'

He smiled broadly showing off neat white teeth and slid casually into the seat next to her own, lowering his voice even though the only other person present was comfortably out of earshot at the far side of the room.

'Your diligence and dedication have not gone unnoticed, and neither have your wealth of other assets, and I'd like to discuss a unique proposition with you tonight, if that's okay? The only condition is that if you accept, then you must promise to exercise complete discretion, and tell absolutely nobody else about it for now.'

He placed subtle emphasis on the words 'assets', 'proposition' and 'discretion' as he spoke, testing the water and allowing for possible naivety. If it all backfired then she would simply assume that he was fishing for some extra-marital entertainment and turn him down flat, and then he'd walk away and choose another companion instead.

'I'd very much like to hear your suggestions,' she replied instead, and rested her slim hand on the top of his thigh underneath the desk, maintaining steady eye contact and smiling considerably less shyly now, just for him.

Chapter 30

I'd not really planned it, but when I finally left Lee's place I wasn't yet in the mood to tackle Emily back at home and I soon found myself walking along Hallie's road. As her neat red brick house came into view I saw Mike and one of the boys out on the drive washing the car, Mike accidentally-on-purpose spraying the bare-chested boy with the hosepipe and then ducking out of the way as a sponge was thrown in retaliation. The scene was pleasant and peaceful, so utterly removed from my world at the moment that I briefly entertained the thought of turning back around, but then Mike looked up and spotted me, waving me over with a loud and cheery 'good morning.'

'Hallie's just headed to the shops for milk, but she'll be back pretty soon so you've only got a couple of minutes to try to seduce me if you find yourself overcome by desire at the sight of my manly torso!'

He hugged me tightly, grinning, and then let go to ruffle his son's wavy brown hair, sending him on his way to put the kettle on.

'Cute as you are, I'll try to restrain myself this time for Hallie's sake.'

I replied, starting to feel slightly more like a human being again after my late morning walk.

'Come on, let's go inside and I'll sort out coffee; I would suggest something stronger, but I think you already beat me to that one.'

He turned and led the way indoors and I realised I was grateful for the chance to get back in out of the sun, since it was beginning to feel like intense dehydration looming large again.

'Guilty as charged, Mike. Don't suppose I could get a vat of water to go with that coffee too, please?'

I grimaced sheepishly and he nodded as he disappeared from view to organise the drinks, whistling loudly and tunelessly and clanking cups together as he did so.

No sooner had he walked out then Hallie arrived back looking effortlessly immaculate in a cream coloured maxi dress and a sparkly headband that matched her painted finger and toenails. I found myself contemplating how you can easily go off a person.

'Woah there! No offence Webby, but you look like you went swimming in a barrel of gin last night! What's up?'

She handed milk to Mike when he emerged briefly at the sound of her voice and he kissed her gently as he took it from her, and then leaned over to pass me a large glass of water.

'Thank you. I owe it all to a heavy and eventful night laden down with sister trouble.'

She shared a look of sympathy and took a seat opposite me.

'Want to talk about it hun?'

'Maybe later. I actually wanted to run some ideas about the murder investigation past you while I sober up away from Emily. Sorry, I know it's not exactly the most pleasant choice of conversational matter for a social call that you'll get this week, but I don't want to go back there yet and my minds running in circles as ever. I've already been over to Lee's this morning, and he's so disgustingly fresh and cheerful that I might just have killed him if I'd stayed in his company for another minute.'

I tried on a weak smile and she turned her body to face me properly, pulling her feet up onto the chair and crossing her legs. Mike arrived right on cue with coffee, handing each of us a mug and sitting to one side with a newspaper, leaving us to get on with it.

'Okay, I'm not sure exactly how much use I can be with something like this, but fire away. What have you got that you're allowed to tell us so far?'

She sipped from her mug, keeping her eyes fixed on me.

'Well, I'm working on the theory that this one knows me somehow. That he's crossed my path in the past, and that's what's behind him leaving me these letters at the scenes. The only problem with that is that I've arrested an awful lot of nasty characters, anyone of which could be the one that we're looking for, and in the absence of anything meaningful from forensics so far I need some kind of criteria for reducing their number.'

I blew on my own coffee and risked a small sip as Mike surprised us all by speaking up first.

'If you don't mind me butting in for a minute, why exactly are you just focussing on the criminals that you've met?' He said.

97

Chapter 31

'What do you mean?'

We both looked over at him for an explanation as he casually folded the newspaper and rested it on the arm of his chair.

'Just that it's difficult to see how that fits with your theory in some respects.' He sat up straighter and leaned forward in the seat. 'I mean, when you discount the obvious fact that many of them are going to be violent and criminally inclined, it looks less likely that one of them is going to be your man without him really sticking out in your mind in some way. After all, if you're so meaningful to him that he's writing to you and only you at these scenes, then you'd have to assume that there's, in his mind at least, a much bigger connection going on than just the fact that you locked him up once for something relatively minor. It would have to be fairly minor or he'd still be in prison.'

He paused and took a sip of coffee, looking deep in thought.

'Unless, of course, there was some kind of resonance that I just didn't pick up on at the time, or they felt I was somehow to blame for something bigger that I'm not aware of, or I've never met them at all and they're just a common garden variety psycho with a fixation.' I ventured, sighing in frustration. 'This is hopeless isn't it? I'm trying to attach logic and reasoning to the actions of somebody whose perception of those two concepts is as different from mine as night is from day.'

I fussed with my hair and Mike wagged a finger at me, tutting exaggeratedly.

'I'm no detective, in fact all of my knowledge on police investigations comes from books and films and listening to you, so your experience and knowledge trumps mine every time Zara. But my point is that this freak might actually know you, and not just be somebody who you've arrested.'

He paused for a moment to let that opinion settle in before carrying on.

'I'm willing to bet that most crims don't even remember the faces of the police officers who arrest them, much less their names and how their careers have progressed. I'm pretty sure that serial killers with vendettas don't tend to exist outside of Hollywood movies. What I'm saying is that, to begin with at least, your list needs to be much bigger.'

His expression was open and serious, and I found myself wondering for the first time how much he and Hallie had been discussing the case that had been eating me up for so long now that I could barely remember life before it.

'We can both help you to narrow down the list once you've got it all together, no matter how big a job it is.'

Hallie stood up and manoeuvred her way around the coffee table between us, embracing me tightly while I leaned in gratefully.

'I love you, you know?'

I mumbled into her shoulder.

'I love you too. Now for God's sake go and make it up with Emily and then get some sleep, the fumes coming off you are making me tipsy. When you're feeling vaguely sober again start adding names to that list – ex-boyfriends, people you fell out with years ago, even male colleagues.'

She paused and let go of me, waiting for a reaction to the suggestion that another police officer could be responsible for these atrocities.

'It's alright, the thought had crossed my mind already, repellent as the idea is I can't afford to be sentimental about it.'

I massaged my temples in a vain attempt to soothe away the returning headache.

'And I'd better see my name on there too, Zara.'

Mike spoke up again and I looked across at him quizzically.

'I'm male and I've known you for a long time, that's enough to put me on that list until it can be demonstrated that I shouldn't be. No omissions.'

Chapter 32

Elizabeth Josephine Perry moved around her small bedroom performing an elated mock waltz. Her thick, lustrous hair was still wet from the shower and it clung to her naked body as she twirled and tossed her towel aside. She looked at herself in the full length mirror on the back of her wardrobe door and liked what she saw. Contrary to the opinions of her colleagues back in the office, 'Shy Beth' was not the demure little girl that they evidently believed her to be. She blew the twin in the reflection a kiss and reached for her moisturiser, enjoying the chocolate aroma of the body butter as she smoothed it into her flawless skin.

'This show needs music.'

She told herself aloud, leaning across to flick on her battered old CD player. If tonight went how she thought it would then she'd be able to buy an upgrade before the week was out. Right away Florence and the Machine's 'Howl' filled the room.

'I hunt for you with bloody feet across the hallowed ground.'

She mimicked the atmospheric wailing passably well while she painted her nails in a shade of bright red polish that always reminded her of jelly beans. When she was happy that her fingers and toes were dry enough she started attending to her make up and hair. Opting for a couple of easily removable strategically placed clips after she'd finished drying and straightening, with red lip gloss and subtle smoky eye shadow on her face. By the time that she'd finished attending to herself and started to put on her favourite little black dress, the album was moving towards its conclusion and Florence was mournfully singing about coffins and death.

Elizabeth had met men of all varieties, shapes and sizes through the internet before, keeping those experiences strictly to herself since she was perfectly adept at splitting her life into entirely separate secret compartments. Most of the one's she'd met had assumed that she was exactly what she had chosen to present to them, and she relished playing the different roles that her fertile imagination invented. However, some of them had been playing roles of their own too, which was why she carried an illegally obtained twenty thousand volt stun gun in her handbag. Truth be told she'd used it more often than had been strictly necessary in the past.

She snapped back out of her thoughts and gave herself one more appraising glance in the mirror, picking a couple of stray pieces of lint off the fabric of her dress. Pretty good, and she had to be tonight. This one was the big one, her possible ticket to a much more comfortable life than this for both herself and her mother. For somebody so adept at weaving fantasies, she was a realist on what counted, and she was under no illusions that he would be in a hurry to leave his wife and risk losing half of his considerable wealth for her anytime soon. Sheds make it clear that she was just fine with that, subject to a couple of conditions of course, when the time was right.

She stopped at her mother's room on her way out of the door, reminding her for the tenth time that evening that she was going out on a date with a wealthy older man and kissing the frail but not yet elderly woman on the cheek. She had no problem with sharing the titbit despite her soon to be companions instructions that she should not, because she knew for a fact that the information would drift back out of her mother's memory again like smoke in the wind before she had even caught her bus.

Chapter 33

When I arrived home Emily was back in super chef mode, busily preparing a banquet for lunch that would have comfortably fed a rugby team by the looks of it. She swayed merrily from side to side in time to Lady Gaga's 'Bad Romance', with no apparent concept of irony, while she worked. She remained oblivious to my presence in the kitchen doorway until the song came to an end, and when she finally caught sight of me in her peripheral vision she flinched in surprise before she caught herself and smiled awkwardly.

'Before you say anything, I just want to apologise for last night, Zara. I had far too much to drink, not that it's a decent excuse for...what I did.'

She shifted awkwardly from one foot to the other and stirred some kind of fragrant garlicky sauce with the wooden spoon she was clutching.

'Anyway, I wanted to try to make it up to you, or to start making it up anyway. Now you go sit down, and I'll shout up when it's ready.'

She spoke rapidly and breathlessly throughout, giving me no chance to interject, and I was left struck by how manic she seemed and wondering how I'd missed it in her behaviour before. I tried to get a closer look at her eyes, but she was moving around too much for me to get a clear enough view, so I retreated to the living room with a tornado of questions whirling round my head.

'So what are we having today?'

I raised my voice up high enough for her to hear me comfortably over the noise of furiously bubbling pans, scratching around for a decision on what to do about her odd demeanour.

'It's spaghetti a la puttanesca with insalata tricolore and home-made garlic and oregano bread. David's been getting me to make it all the time recently, it's one of his favourites. We had it three times the other week!' Came back the reply.

I felt a growing sense of steadily worsening unease, both at the strained sense of cheerfulness saturating her voice, and at the strange snippet of information that she'd just shared with me. It's no secret that spaghetti a la puttanesca roughly translates as 'whore's spaghetti', a fact that I couldn't imagine was lost on Emily. She was, despite all appearance to the contrary, an intelligent, articulate and educated woman like me, and I began to have serious concerns that the current obvious difficulties in her marriage might be built around his growing suspicions about her indiscretions. Who the hell gets his wife to make a dish named after prostitutes three times in a week if he's not trying to make a point?

'If he knew then he'd kill me... actually murder me...' I remembered her drunken words from last night and tried not to put too much stock in them, after all, it wasn't at all unusual for people to express those kinds of sentiments and not really mean them. Hell, I'd even told Hallie how I might have killed Lee earlier, and I was beginning to love him deeply. The bad feeling refused to budge though, and in light of everything else that was happening I didn't want to dismiss my worries about her safety lightly.

Emily's handbag was perched beside her chair with an empty

wineglass leaning against it. I took a quick glance up at the doorway and moved over in a crouch, not sure what I expected to find if I looked inside. My timing could not have been any worse if I'd tried. I flipped open the clasp, and after a brief rummage around, my hand emerged with a small cardboard packet labelled 'Prozac', and at that precise moment my baby sister walked right in and caught me red handed.

Chapter 34

'What the hell are you doing in my bag?'

All trace of good humour vanished from Emily's face in an instant, and she stood frozen in place with two plates of steaming food in her hands, staring at me as rage started to creep across her features.

Now that she was no longer moving around I could clearly see the dilation of her pupils, so I had to assume that she'd washed down the antidepressants with more than just one glass of wine today.

'I'm sorry, I shouldn't have gone through your bag without your permission. But I'm really worried about you Em. Your moods and behaviour have been all over the place ever since you arrived, and some of what you said last night made me scared for your safety.'

I kept my tone neutral and tried to avoid too much direct eye contact, automatic reflexes when you've already served half of what is considered to be a full term in the police force. I still wasn't convinced that I could diffuse the situation with all the history that lay between us, but I wanted to try at least.

'So you thought you'd just go through my things anyway? My personal, private things, rather than letting me talk to you in my own time. Even after I told you that I came here because I trusted you not to pry?'

She didn't shout but I could hear the accusation and venom in her voice. It wasn't difficult to look at the situation through her eyes, I'd just let her down very badly indeed.

'It wasn't supposed...'

I started an attempt at an explanation but she cut me off immediately.

'Spare me your pathetic reasons for Christ's sake.'

I could see furious tears starting to well up in the corners of her unfocussed eyes, and she blinked hard several times to try to clear them away.

'Well I hope you're truly happy now you've unravelled the mystery and discovered that your baby sister is a fucking lunatic? Use whatever words you like. Unstable, depressive, insane, not to be trusted with her own children in case those dark little voices inside her head compel her to do something unspeakable.'

Her pretty face was twisted up into a sneer of sheer hatred, some of it directed at me, but seemingly most of it being directed squarely at herself. I found myself overwhelmed with guilt that she had landed on my doorstep in what was clearly a cry for help, and I'd been so wrapped up in my work and my own comparatively happy life that I'd not even noticed.

'Emily, I am so, so sorry; I had no idea how much you were hurting and what was going on. If you'd only told me on the phone or when you arrived then I could have been more supportive. I could have tried to help.'

I stepped towards her and the anger flared up in her again as she bared her teeth at me in warning like an animal.

'I didn't want you making allowances for me, I didn't want you to do what everybody else is doing and start treating me like some kind of MADWOMAN.'

She was shouting now, starting to lose what little self control she still possessed. I stretched out my arms towards her but she backed away.

'No Zara, it's far too late for that now. I'm leaving and I'll never see you again after today. But here's something to remember me by.'

Without further warning she launched both plates of spaghetti in my direction, spattering me and the carpets and furniture with scolding hot pasta sauce.

Chapter 35

Elizabeth could see that he was impressed from the moment that he arrived to pick her up from the kerbside on a quiet country lane. His expression remained friendly and neutral, but he was unable to prevent himself running a lingering gaze over every inch of her like a caress. She understood his desire for discretion and was happy enough to respect it too, but a small part of her had been irritated at having to walk right out the far end of town and half a mile along a dirt track in her best heels. Of course that part had swiftly disappeared when his brand new silver Jaguar glided into view. The car was a thing of beauty, and she'd slid easily into the electronically warmed passenger seat and savoured the newness of the aromas – leather, polish and pine air freshener – that saturated the air inside.

'My apologies for the choice of meeting place. I trust that the walk wasn't too much of an inconvenience for you?'

His voice was deep and full, not a trace of the infirmity of age, although she guessed that he was probably older than her mother, who looked practically ancient by comparison due to the ravages of her illnesses.

'Actually there was a point halfway up this track when I cursed the fact that I hadn't worn my trainers, but at least you didn't leave me standing and waiting for long.'

She worked hard to keep the ghost of petulance out of her words and finished the sentence with a dazzling smile.

'In that case I'll need to work extra hard to make it up to you tonight then, won't I?'

He returned the smile casually and waited for her to clip in the seatbelt before he pulled smoothly away.

'So do I have to wait until we arrive at wherever you're taking me before you share any details of this opportunity, or are you going to give me some little teasers on the way?'

She looked over at him, fluttering her eyelashes playfully when he risked a glance back.

'I always find that anticipation heightens the experience in life, but you'll be finding out soon enough.'

He faced forwards again looking thoroughly pleased with himself and Elizabeth found herself thinking about the stun gun momentarily again.

'How do you know that I'll like it when I do find out?' she asked innocently, noticing that he was concentrating more on their surroundings than on her now and wondering how often he'd done this kind of thing before.

'Because I know what I want and I know what you want to, and between us I know that we can be part of something special.'

He guided the Jaguar around a tight turn to the right, heading right up into the hills and woodland, and the conversation died away for a few minutes. Elizabeth turned her face to the window to hide her disappointment from him, making a pretence of looking out at the view. Earlier in the day she'd been dwelling on thoughts of a fine hotel with champagne and a big bed, not some leafy glade in the open air with bugs flying around and thorns scratching up her legs.

Still, if it got her what she wanted then she'd endure it this time around.

'Since I can see your scowl in reflected in the window, I'll just let you in on the fact there's a cottage further along this track, and it's got all of the usual creature comforts.'

His voice shocked her back out of her thoughts and she blushed, and turned back towards him, pasting on a guilty look as she mentally kicked herself.

'I'm sorry. I was deep in thought and I tend to scowl when I'm thinking. Anywhere that you take me will be absolutely fine.'

She moved her hand across to rest on his thigh for the second time that day and felt the faint quiver of excitement rippling just under the surface of his skin. All was not lost. She was quite sure that he'd forget all about her little slip when they were in the cottage together alone at last.

Chapter 36

I let Emily go in the aftermath of our argument, in considerable pain where the tomato based sauce had touched my bare arms and neck, and not entirely trusting myself to keep my anger at her actions in check if I followed her out into the street. The carpets were probably ruined, but I was more concerned about the burns on my body anyway, so I stripped and had a long cold shower before liberally applying cold antiseptic cream to soothe my tender skin. I had nothing else to get dressed back up for, so I put on some old pyjamas and wrapped my white dressing gown around myself, pulling my hair back away from my face and then twisting it into a wet ponytail.

When I calmed down enough to go back downstairs and surveyed the mess I almost burst into tears. Livid orange stains coated every available surface, with spaghetti and sauce clinging to cushions, carpets, walls and paintings all around the room. It seemed as if the portions had multiplied once they were liberated from the plates, and the damage could easily run into thousands if I ended up having to replace pictures, furniture and the carpets themselves. As sorry as I'd felt for Emily's situation before and as guilty as I'd been of failing to be there for her this time, I didn't feel like I deserved this, and hot tears started to run down my face.

I'd bought my house three years ago as a new build, and while it wasn't exactly palatial, it was a good sized three bedroom semi in a nice area that I'd lovingly decorated myself and filled with objects that

I adored. I looked up at one of the ruined paintings on the wall, an oil on canvas picture of a glowing red sunset done by a friend who had since died younger than anybody should have to of a quiet cancer that she'd chosen not to tell anybody else about. I'd never be able to replace it, and I'd never be able to forgive Emily for defacing it and in turn Siobhan's memory with it.

Wiping at my cheeks with a fluffy sleeve I made my way through to the kitchen and dragged out the box full of cleaning products, running a bowl full of hot soapy water to take through with me. I might not be able to make it all perfect again, but I could try to rescue some of it as a part measure. Hopefully it would distract me from the ugly emotions that were circling so I could pull myself back together, and if Emily had any good sense left in her head at all she'd stay away and leave me to it. As I carried the full bowl back through, I quietly vowed to have nothing to do with her ever again.

Twenty minutes later I was making much better progress into the big clean up than I'd anticipated, and I'd turned on some music to keep me company while I worked. On closer inspection Siobhan's picture had been treated with some kind of hard-wearing lacquer after she'd finished it, which had protected it from the worst of the damage. There'd be some small red and orange stains left behind, but they wouldn't stand out too much against the other similar colours in the paint. The carpets were another story and were pretty much completely ditched, but I was so pleased about the painting that I could live what that as a trade off. I stood back and looked around the room again, scouting for stray bits of pasta and spotting another strand relaxing on top of a cushion.

As satisfied as I could be for the time being I moved the bowl of dirty water and stained cloths back through onto the kitchen worktop, realising as I did that I'd still not eaten and feeling my stomach growling. The Italian salad of tomatoes, mozzarella and basil was still sitting over to one side, and I knew that I had cooked chicken breast still in the fridge which would do for now. A bottle of some dark coloured liquid with a fancy label that was standing next to the hob turned out to be balsamic vinegar, which I drizzled over the salad after I'd arranged some on a plate with the chicken. The food looked good, and I was beginning to feel marginally better already. I'd almost managed to sit down and get the first forkful up to my mouth when the doorbell rang and my body dumped adrenaline into my bloodstream in anticipation of another fight.

Chapter 37

It was immediately obvious as I entered the hallway that the figure behind the front door wasn't Emily. Even in silhouette it was too tall and stocky to be female, and as it turned its head to the side I caught the outline of glasses on its face. I hesitated for a moment, not immediately recognising the figure behind opaque glass, as they rang the bell in impatience for a second time. Whoever it was they weren't going to go away without talking to me, it seemed, so I inserted the key and opened up the door.

'David. What are you doing in these parts?'

My heart sank as my sister's husband fixed me with his unpleasant stare, curling up one corner of his mouth in a gesture that I imagine was supposed to be a smile of greeting, but which fell a long way short. It was no secret that I was not his biggest fan.

'Where is Emily?'

His tone was clipped and arrogant, the accent advertising that he had been

educated and raised the expensive way somewhere much further South than

Coventry. As ever he wasn't going to bother with pleasantries and expected me to just tell him what he wanted upon command so he could go back to more important business.

'The last time I checked she was married to you. You tell me where she is?'

I wasn't playing, especially after what she'd told me about his demeanour towards her. If she wanted to be found then she'd call him to come and fetch her as far as I was concerned.

'She's been somewhat...distracted recently, and we agreed to have some time apart for her to rest. Unfortunately she's been ignoring my calls and messages since she left, which has necessitated me having to track her down.'

His body language and facial expression told me what his words didn't. This was all a big inconvenience and an embarrassment for him and he was acting on that basis rather than out of genuine concern for Emily's welfare. It seemed like this was merely about saving face to him, and I felt the residual anger from the earlier argument starting to rise back up to dangerous levels again.

'Didn't you even consider for one moment speaking to the rest of her family about what condition she was in before now? Do you even really care about her or anybody else at all for that matter?'

I was ranting a little and I knew it, but a tiny part of me wanted to provoke a response, so I could see for myself the darkness in him that Emily had spoken about.

'So you have seen her then?'

His eyes narrowed and I found myself wishing that I'd chosen my words more carefully.

'She's not here now, David. I don't know where she is. But even if I did you'd be among the very last people that I'd feel inclined to share that information with.'

I glared at him in case he was still in any doubt that I thought he was pond life.

'That's disappointing,' he said, and suddenly shot out his arms, pushing me hard enough to send me reeling back into my hallway and catching me completely off guard. I tried to grab onto something for balance, but my momentum sent me tumbling to the floor and he was in before I could jam my feet against the door.

'EMILY? IF YOU'RE IN HERE IT WOULD BE IN YOUR INTERESTS TO COME OUT RIGHT NOW.'

His shouting filled my ears in the confined space and I fought to get back to my feet until he placed his foot in the middle of my chest and pushed my back down again.

I was about to begin shouting myself when David lurched violently backwards out of my view and out through the front door, letting out a startled roar as he went. Pushing myself up into a sitting position again I caught sight of the blur of Lee's fist as he drove it into David's doubled up body over and over again.

Chapter 38

The cottage looked infinitely better than the prospect of rolling around on a picnic blanket in the great outdoors had been. Elizabeth admired the green wooden shutters that matched the front door and the way that the surrounding woodland seemed to embrace the small stone building protectively, and she started to imagine what it might be like to live up here away from the clutter of the town. She didn't mind the fact that her silver haired companion had grown increasingly quiet as they had moved away from civilisation, she wasn't a big fan of small talk at the best of times, and if he was getting nervy and thinking about backing out she was confident that she could get him back on track in a matter of moments.

He looked over and held eye contact with her as he located the front door key and opened up, standing aside like a gentleman should to allow her to enter first. She smiled and trailed her hand down his cheek as she passed, trying to compute the significance of the fierce intensity in his eyes which was at odds with the rest of his facial expression, and feeling a small seed of disquiet in her stomach.

'You can relax, you know? We've got as much time as we need and I'm not about to tell anybody about this.'

She talked over her shoulder while she explored the space inside, mindful of his feelings and not wanting to make him feel threatened.

'Yes. I know,' was all he could manage in reply, his voice hoarser than usual.

Everything was tastefully decorated, with an open living and dining area, separate country style kitchen, and steep stairs leading off the hallway up to what she assumed must be the bedrooms and bathroom upstairs. She wandered through the living room first. A fire was burning in the grate, so presumably he'd headed up here before coming to collect her. A chunky oak coffee table sat before the fire in front of an antique-looking leather settee big enough to accommodate several people, and behind the settee was a modest dining table with places set for two. She dropped her handbag onto one of the chairs.

'This is very nice.'

She turned back towards him, feeling his presence at her shoulder and catching him staring at her. Outwardly tactful person that she was, she pretended not to notice and ran her hand over a furry throw resting on the back of the chair.

'Thank you. May I fix you a drink? There's champagne cooling in the kitchen.'

He seemed to be snapping back out of his weird fugue and remembering his manners at least, but she still felt the awkwardness like a weight pressing down on them both.

'You sit back and I'll pour the drinks, sometimes it's nice to let a woman take charge.'

She winked at him and guided him down into the chair gently, feeling him tense and then relent and relax.

The kitchen was compact but pretty, with a Belfast sink inset into a solid wood worktop, and flowers in a vase on the window sill. The champagne flutes were standing right next to the bottle chilling in a silver ice bucket, but much of the ice had already started to melt. She removed the cork with ease, being no stranger to bar work from her college days, and decided to look for fresh ice while she was in here. The split stable door to the left must be where the fridge-freezer lived since there was no sign of any food in here.

'ARE YOU OKAY THROUGH THERE?'

He sounded slightly anxious and tense and she wondered idly whether he was planning dessert without the dinner, with the champagne to seal the deal.

'YES, COMING IN A MINUTE, JUST FETCHING...ice...'

The volume of her voice dropped to a whisper on the last word as she pushed open the door through into the 'utility' room and saw what was inside. The space was almost empty, with only a large ceiling hook, a bench saw and an industrial looking machine that she didn't recognise sitting in the middle of the floor. The walls and ceiling appeared to have been freshly repainted, but strange dark stains still showed through.

'It's for mincing up large portions of meat.'

His voice came from right behind her ear, unmistakeably low and menacing, and her heart rate accelerated as she began to put all of the pieces together in her head and quietly wished that she hadn't left the bag with her stun gun in the other room.

Chapter 39

After Lee had taken David away and I had stopped shaking again I opened up a bottle of Chianti and poured myself a deep glass, then grabbed a pen and a pad of paper and sat down to write. Lee had wanted to stay with me, but after I'd explained about the cream on my neck and arms and assured him that I was doing just fine and planning an early night, he'd finally relented. I'd made him promise not to take a bloodied and bruised David into custody, despite his uninvited entry into my home, on the basis that his injuries would prompt questions that could result in big trouble for Lee. He'd only agreed after explaining to David in painstaking detail what his fate would be if he ever pulled a stunt like that again, and that he needed to thank me copiously for intervening before he'd gotten into a proper rhythm.

I tried to block the image of David pushing his way into my home with his face twisted into a mask of cold rage, and I tried even harder to push away the humiliation I felt about how powerless I'd been sprawled out on the floor in my own hallway with his heavy foot on my chest. I needed to do something more constructive than drinking a whole bottle of wine today, if I wanted to start convincing myself that I could catch the Grey Man before he decided to do something horrifying to yet another unsuspecting victim. I won't forget what you did though, David. I'm not Emily, not by a long chalk, and I'll make sure you know how it felt to be in my position today.

I took a big gulp of wine and flipped open the pad to a fresh page to resurrect the list of male names that I'd begun to collate for my suspects list. Fred Russell had agreed without question to my earlier call asking for a list of arrests of white males that I'd made since starting up with the Warwickshire police force. That fact was in itself slightly disturbing. Fred questioned everything I did as a general rule, and we'd already pretty much ruled out this line of enquiry earlier in the investigation. Not that I was about to start digging deeper into the reasons for his sudden new strand of leniency.

After some consideration and another few swallows of wine, I started with guys from my university days, reasoning that towards the end of my degree I'd all but decided to pursue a career with the police, so it was just about feasible that some of them might have remembered that fact after all this time. The list of ex-boyfriends from that time was disappointingly brief. I'd been awkward and shy around men until I hit my mid twenties – the 'rugby' years as I now thought of them, when I'd courted a taste for slightly older bearish guys – so I dropped in a couple of names that I remembered as casual acquaintances and friends for good measure, in order to avoid the inevitable mockery from Hallie later.

I stopped and headed to the kitchen for a refill, hesitating and then bringing the whole bottle back through to keep me company. I could always screw the lid back on what was left when I was done, I kidded myself. The rugby years were trickier, not that I'd been more active than most of the women that I'd known back then, but because what guys had featured had not been especially significant to me. I finished off the modest list of lovers and boyfriends, there'd been very few once my career had began to take off, and started to drop in the names of anybody else with an unsavoury reputation that came to mind.

I sat back and began to read over the growing list but unfortunately nobody really leapt out at me as a potential serial killing cannibal, so it looked like I was going to have to do it the methodical way. I was about to put it aside for the night when I recalled Mike and Hallie's words, and jotted down Mike's name along with David's and several of the male officers that I'd partnered or worked alongside at various stages, feeling horrible as I did so. I stopped at the last line on the page, my pen hovering as I drained the rest of my glass of wine and considered. Finally I scribbled down the name anyway, reasoning that it was too stupid to even consider and that he'd probably just laugh it off if I told him anyway. Lee was my best friend, partner in crime, or crime prevention anyway, and obviously above suspicion. I'd be able to discreetly scrub him back off again in no time at all, and he'd never even have to know about it.

Chapter 40

The day didn't start out feeling like it would be full of tragedy and pain. The sun was shining brightly enough to wake me up naturally before my alarm sounded, and it was already warm enough for me to take breakfast out onto the little suntrap patio area that served as my back garden by the time that I'd showered and changed.

The previous day's events seemed vague and unreal against the backdrop of singing birds and soft floral scents that permeated the breeze, and I felt something like normal again. Reinvigorated by the sunshine and realising how early it still was, I weighed up my options. Finally deciding to change into leggings and a vest top and fit in a short run over the other option of getting into the office even earlier than usual. I figured that after yesterday's events I could take some me time without guilt, and I already pulled in more hours than virtually anybody else in CID anyway.

Ten minutes later I was entering the cool shade of birch and cedar trees in the country park, feeling surprisingly fresh considering the bottle of wine that I'd drunk last night. Startled squirrels chattered angrily at me as I passed, scampering up high into the canopy until I was safely out of sight again, and unseen small creatures rustled in the thick leaf litter. I'd forgotten my mp3 on my way out of the door, but I soon drifted into a comfortable rhythm and zoned out, inhabiting that special runner's place where you feel like you could run effortlessly forever.

It was as I emerged at the far end of the trail that I was pulled back out of my Zen state by the vibration of my phone in my pocket. Here the woodland gave way to twin tarmac drives leading up to a large country house hotel, and, after that, sloped down towards the edge of a large housing estate that cannibalised yet another patch of the idyllic surroundings each time the council relented and granted more planning permission. I slowed to a fast walk, cooling down while I fumbled for my suddenly evasive mobile.

'Wade.'

A call at this time of the morning was going to be business related, so I dispensed with any attempt at a more extended greeting.

'Erm... hello? I'm trying to get hold of a Zara Wade... is this her?'

The person calling was thrown by the curt manner in which I'd answered, and I backpedalled, dropping the office voice in recognition that this was definitely not work after all.

'Sorry, I thought you might be work. Yes, this is Zara Wade, how can I help?'

My mind raced through possibilities in the fraction of a second before the reply came.

'My name's Doctor Rashid, Ms Wade, I work at the University Hospital Coventry and I've been looking after your sister Emily.'

He paused to allow me to absorb some of the information and I stepped straight in.

'What's happened to her? Is she okay?'

I could feel my resolution to have nothing more to do with her melting away as I tried not to panic about what might have

126

happened.

'She's asleep at present, but her condition is stable. We believe that she took a deliberate overdose of antidepressants late last night, but thankfully she made a phone call to the emergency services before it was too late, and we're optimistic that the damage to her major organs won't be severe when she comes back around.'

He delivered the news in a matter of fact but warm fashion, and I thanked him for his call and received permission to call in later in the day when visiting hours were open.

I put the phone back in my pocket feeling utterly numb with shock and started jogging again, but at a much slower pace than before. I mentally ran back over as much of my actions from the previous night as I could recall, looking for any sign that I might have missed that she was going to do something this stupid, but drew a blank. Angry, hurt and betrayed, yes, majorly pissed off too, but not suicidal, not when she'd left me anyway. This couldn't be my doing, there had to be more to it than that, didn't there? I stopped and took my phone back out again and rang Lee.

Chapter 41

'Hi there gorgeous, I'm taking it that you've heard, too, then?'

Lee's deep voice filled my ear through the receiver and immediately confused the hell out of me.

'You know already? But why would they tell you before they told me?'

I was deeply upset at the revelation, trying to understand what else could have happened for other people to learn about it before me.

'Of course, the whole station knows about it by now I imagine, I figured I'd tell you when you arrived. I didn't think it would affect you quite like this though, I have to admit.'

His voice was hesitant now as he recognised the hurt in my tone.

'Why the hell would I not be upset at that? She's MY bloody sister but apparently I'm the last to know anything as usual.'

It came out as a cross between a hiss and a shout, but I didn't care about the venom, I felt fully entitled to be aggrieved in this situation.

'Wait. We're obviously talking about two different things here. You're saying that something's happened to Emily?'

His voice was suddenly full of concern and empathy.

'Yes, she took an overdose last night. I've just got off the phone to the hospital. I thought for a minute that...what were you talking about?'

I shook my head, involuntarily trying to rid myself of the residue of frustration and anger from the last twenty four hours that had started to cling to me again.

'I am so sorry, Zara. My news was about Fred Russell, he suffered a heart attack on the golf course yesterday afternoon, managed to survive it even though they didn't find him for a while, but it's looking like the end of his career anyway. It's the talk of the station, of course, but that can wait. Did they say how Emily's bearing up at the moment, or give any indication of what sparked it?'

The last question was a loaded one. He knew that I'd be blaming myself after the big row with her before she ran out.

'They think she'll be pretty much fine but that's all I've been told so far. Do you know if Fred's allowed visitors? I'm going to be up at the hospital later this afternoon with Emily and I'd like to stop in, if he's up to it.'

Actually, if I was really honest with myself, I was much more comfortable with the idea of visiting him than my sister. I was also growing well and truly flustered as I recognised the implications of Fred Russell's illness. Without him around I was the most senior detective in the department, which theoretically put me in charge. It wasn't surprising that nobody else had broken their neck to come and tell me about what had happened; I was now 'the boss'.

'I can find out for you. Enough about everybody else though, how are you managing this morning? You do know that what she chose to do isn't your fault right?'

I could picture him with grey eyes full of concern and I started to choke up.

'Yes, I know. I'm okay...or I will be anyway. Just find something for us to do when I get in that doesn't involve me having to sit around to be gawped at by all and sundry.'

I stifled a sob at the end.

'Will do. I love you Zara.'

He said and ended the call.

I started up walking, needing to get home to freshen up a second time this morning, and a greying collie dog strolled leisurely out of one of the driveways to watch me curiously, ducking back in out of reach when I drew level. In the last dozen hours or so I'd been burned with hot food, attacked by my sister's husband, considered my boyfriend as a possible murder suspect, and received news that my sister had tried to kill herself. Now my boss had keeled over too. What better set of circumstances could there be to take on the biggest promotion of my career right in the middle of a seemingly unsolvable serial murder case?

'Shit Wade, you never take the easy route in life do you?'

I muttered under my breath, and began to force the pace again, relocating my resolve and wiping at my eyes with the back of my hand.

Chapter 42

When I arrived at the station Lee was already out in the car park waiting for me, with the mild breeze ruffling up his blond hair and pushing his pink tie over to one side. As I joined him he quickly briefed me on a possible development in the Grey Man case and handed over the keys to an unmarked Volvo together with a scribbled down note of the address. he knows me well enough by now to be aware that I prefer to drive than be driven.

'It could be absolutely nothing, but a girl called Elizabeth Perry has gone missing from her home near Nuneaton and she matches a similar physical type to the others. She lives with her mother, but the home help reported her gone when she arrived to take over with mum's care in the morning and there was nobody to let her in.'

I looked at him quizzically as I unlocked the car and we both climbed inside.

'The mother has dementia and needs a lot of supervision, but Elizabeth works in the day so they have an assistant in to help out. The helper says the girl is fastidious to a fault, never gone AWOL without letting anybody know before.'

I started the engine and cruised slowly up to the car park barrier, waiting for the receptionist to raise it up for us.

'What sort of age are we talking about for Elizabeth?'

The barrier lifted and I turned left, heading out towards the motorway.

'She's nineteen, a clerk for some kind of IT security company, very pretty apparently, but shy and keeps to herself according to the helper. She's not affluent like some of the others, so we'll have to reconsider the whole society angle if it is him.'

I glanced over and he looked lost in thought, we both knew that descriptions of character by others generally only reveal one facet of a person's behaviour.

'Let's hope not for now, shall we? With any luck she just got overwhelmed playing nursemaid and went out to let off some steam for once. She wouldn't be the first teenager to do so.'

My words sounded hollow even to my own ears, but my investigative brain was already counting her among the dead, and working out the possible significance of a victim from a less privileged background than almost all of the others.

'Do you think this is going to be a waste of time?'

He was referring to us having a chat with mum and the helper, since the mother's condition was likely to make her of no use whatsoever. If Elizabeth was off gallivanting then she wasn't necessarily going to let the carer in on her plans.

'Probably, but I want to get a look at her room, so it might be worth a trip out anyway. Nine times out of ten teenage girls seem to have an irresistible urge to write down their misdemeanours in a diary.'

I flicked on the indicator and drifted off down a side road, taking a route that would keep us away from the busier roads.

'That was before the information revolution. If there's anything dark and dirty in her closet then it'll be out in the blogosphere somewhere under an alias no doubt.'

He pulled a sour face. The internet was both a blessing and a curse for modern police investigations.

'If she's as insular as we're being told then we might get lucky.'

I didn't believe my own statement. If she was a strictly pen and paper girl then she probably wouldn't be working in computing, and the perceived anonymity of the web made it easy for people to forget about how their movements online could be tracked without too much difficulty, but I'm an optimist most of the time so I was clinging to that small hope regardless. Please have left us something to go on Elizabeth.

'You're the boss.'

I caught his cheeky smile in my peripheral vision as I rounded another corner at speed, and despite everything I found myself unable to stop shaking my head in mock dismay and grinning back at him.

Chapter 43

'Mrs Perry is not going to be much help to you I'm afraid.'

Ms Diane Lamb, the 'professional care worker' as she'd referred to herself at least four times in the two minutes since our arrival, directed her speech solely at Lee.

On another day I might have spoken up about her presumption that, as a man, he was automatically the senior officer here; but that assumption and her machine gun style of conversation allowed me the freedom to leave him to deal with her alone while I headed further into the house to explore.

'I'll be back with you in just a minute.' I said, excusing myself and heading upstairs without the woman even acknowledging that I'd spoken.

I avoided the mother's room for now, eager to take a quick look around Elizabeth's personal space unaccompanied, and knowing straight away which bedroom was the girls out of three possible choices from the nameplate on her door. Even without the plaque the scent of perfume and skin products emanating from that section of the house would have left little doubt that this was a younger woman's domain.

There was some resistance as I pushed open the door, but it proved to be nothing more sinister than a discarded bath towel, still slightly damp to the touch. An explosion of cosmetics was randomly arranged on top of an old table, together with a chipped mirror, the two seemed to function as a makeshift dressing table, and on the bed was evidence of a young lady preparing for a very big night out. I lifted the corner of the pile of discarded dresses with a biro, just in case anything in here became of evidential value further down the line. They were at the expensive end of high street, which was at odds with the description of the girl as someone who never socialised. Who were you dressing up for Elizabeth?

Realising that I couldn't risk spending too much time in here before somebody asked where I was and what I was up to, I opened up each of the drawers in a battered old unit in turn, hastily scanning through the contents while trying not to make too much noise. Nothing screamed out 'diary' to me, and the same was true of the interior of the wardrobe, even after I opened up the shoe boxes in the bottom and checked to see whether the board at the base could be lifted out. I stopped for a moment, thinking fast and then deciding on the underneath of the mattress as my best chance. Jackpot. Not a diary, but a username and password for a computer, although there was no sign of one in the bedroom itself. I decided that I'd ridden my luck enough for the time being and pocketed the scrap of paper before exiting leaving everything just as I had found it.

'Elizabeth? Elizabeth? Is that you?'

The voice came from behind the door opposite as I moved back across the landing, making me jump in surprise; the voice of a younger woman than I'd been expecting to hear.

Footsteps approached from downstairs as Diane Lamb heard her calling and began to make her way up, followed by Lee. Forced to improvise, I chose door number three and was relieved to find that it was a bathroom. I flushed the toilet and then switched on the tap for a few seconds, counting to ten before I switched it back off and emerged onto the landing for a second time.

'We're okay to speak to Mrs Perry now.'

Lee eyed me quizzically while the carer pushed past me towards the sound of the ill woman, and I gave him a wink as I turned to follow.

Inside the bedroom was the scent of bleach and disinfectant, but they failed to completely mask the aroma of something rotten underneath. I tried and failed to keep my smile in place for Mrs Perry's benefit, but swiftly realised that it didn't matter since she was virtually oblivious to our presence.

'These two people are friends of Elizabeth's, they just wanted to ask if you know where she's nipped out to Mary?'

Diane tried her best on our behalf, but the sick woman stayed silent.

'Okay, we'll leave it at that for now, Diane. Just let us know if she tells you anything which might help at all later, even if it doesn't seem particularly significant.'

Lee smiled quickly wanting to escape this place sooner rather than later.

'A rich old man to take care of us both,' said Mrs Perry softly and looked up with fierce intensity for a long moment, meeting my brown eyes with her own virtually colourless ones, and then her head drooped back forward again and she was beyond our reach once more.

Chapter 44

I don't suppose that all that many people are particularly fond of visiting hospitals, but I have an especially strong dislike for them that is born out of the unusual amount of time that my job has required me to spend in such places. I walked down the corridors of the University Hospital Coventry without needing to stop and ask anybody for directions. I'd already been told which wards both Emily and Fred Russell were being treated on and the maze of identical hallways no longer held any mysteries for me anymore. I passed signs for endocrinology, cardiology and the ENT – Ear, Nose and Throat clinic – in turn, weaving around the occasional dawdling confused straggler and the roving bands of medical staff striding with single minded intent past them.

Finally, I reached the 'A' wards, designated for those who required varying levels of psychiatric assistance, stopping at a forlorn looking reception area to explain who I was and why I was here to the disinterested young man behind the desk, until he sighed and buzzed me through without attempting a single word of conversation. Psychiatric wards have come a long, long way since the times of the infamous Bedlam Hospital, where the mentally ill were viewed as good entertainment for those who could pay to see them treated like animals, and the corridors were quiet and still.

'Can I help you?'

A severe looking nurse in a grey uniform with white collar and sleeves stepped out in front of me, effectively barring my progress.

Her expression suggested that she had no intention of helping me in any way whatsoever, if it could possibly be avoided.

'I've come to visit my sister, Emily Foster, I believe she was admitted late last night.'

I offered a placatory smile to deflect her suspicious hostility and she regarded me steadily as if weighing up what to tell me.

'She's in a quiet room of her own on the left at the very bottom of this hallway. I'm sure it would be entirely unnecessary for me to tell you that she's in a particularly fragile state at the moment, and that anybody, family or otherwise, causing her distress would swiftly find themselves leaving my ward?'

She carried on past me without waiting for acknowledgement, and I tried to consider what she dealt with every day so as not to feel too aggrieved. I reached Emily's room two dozen echoing paces later and knocked softly before entering.

Emily was awake and sitting up as I walked in, with dark rings around her sunken eyes. She was wearing a cheap hospital night dress and she looked pale, drawn and exhausted, a shadow of her former self. I fumbled for something to say, feeling intensely awkward due to the circumstances of our last conversation and the fight that had followed, and having to look away from her distant watery gaze for fear that I'd burst into tears.

'I know this is probably the most stupid thing to ask you at this minute in time, but how are you feeling?'

I pulled up a blue hard plastic chair, designed to stop visitors getting too comfortable it appeared, and sat down beside her bed, reaching out and taking hold of a limp clammy hand.

'Is there anything I can do for you, Emily?'

I tried again, and she turned to look at me with complete blankness written on her face.

'Please don't tell David.'

Her words came out over dry lips as a hoarse weak whisper.

Chapter 45

When I left Emily to go back to sleep, promising to visit again as soon as possible, I stopped by Superintendent Fred Russell's room and looked in through a window in the door. The big man was deeply asleep, with a forest of tubes and clips connecting him to a large white and grey machine that monitored his vital signs and presumably supported certain vital bodily functions. I hovered for a few minutes, not certain what to do for him and questioning my wisdom in even being here. He'd never been the kind of man to encourage over familiarity between colleagues, and I couldn't imagine that he'd appreciate waking up to find me sitting and holding his hand like I'd done for Emily. Mind made up, I eventually assured myself that I stayed for long enough and left him to rest undisturbed.

Outside it was drizzling lightly and the sun was out shining through the spray. As I arrived back at my car my phone started to ring, the display showing Lee's new personal mobile number again, although I hadn't yet got round to programming it into my contacts list.

'Hello there Detective Sergeant Mead, what can I do for you today?'

I tried my flirtiest tones, craving some semblance of normality to replace the tension that had crept back in owing to the chaos of the last twenty four hours.

'On any other day I'd answer that in full exhaustive detail, Zara, but I'm afraid there's been another letter for you.'

He paused, both of us knew what that meant by now and my heart sank even further.

'Where did they find her this time?'

My voice was flat and quiet as I contemplated the image of strikingly pretty young Elizabeth, still barely more than a child, mutilated, murdered and abandoned by a monster that we couldn't seem to get close to catching.'

'Obviously I have to be careful about what I say over this phone line, so you're going to have to get over to the station for more details. But, suffice to say that while we haven't found her yet, it's really, really bad.'

His careful choice of words told me that there was much more to this one than the others and I felt a hard lump growing in the back of my throat as I got into the car.

'I take it the letter tells us where to find her though?' I asked, starting up the engine and pulling away with a glance in the mirrors, not caring that I shouldn't be driving with my phone still clamped to my ear.

'In a manner of speaking, but it's more complicated than that. I can't say more until I see you, but there's a welcoming committee assembling here.'

He made a small noise down the phone that sounded oddly like he was trying not to be sick. It's really, really bad.

'Okay, I'm on my way to you now, I'll be there in less than fifteen minutes. And Lee, if there's even a small chance that you can do something for her then don't wait for me to get there to give my permission okay? I trust your judgement.'

That's why I've got your name on my unofficial suspects list at home. My mind reminded me, until I pushed the uncomfortable strand of thought away and accelerated out of the hospital grounds, breaking the onsite speed limit all the way.

I weaved neatly in between two busy lanes of traffic and bullied my way across two more in order to be able to cut back across the shortest route towards the city centre, ignoring the aggressive blast of a car horn as I did so. I'd worked some horrific cases together with Lee, some of them involving atrocious, sadistic acts of violence and sexual abuse of minors, but I couldn't think of the last one which had caused my partner's affected cool façade to slip aside. What on earth was I driving back towards?

Chapter 46

Anthropophagy has been with us for much longer than language or even so called organised, civilised society has, Zara. Our ancestors ate their dead relatives as a mark of respect, to assimilate the atoms of the fallen with their own in essence, rather than abandoning their loved ones to the ravenous depredations of wild animals that might go on to develop the 'taste'. It was both practical and spiritual in application.

In times of conflict throughout history man has eaten the fallen enemy for quite different reasons. Seeking to destroy their bodies completely and remove all identifiable traces of them from earth; what greater indignity to have visited upon them than to deny their friends and relatives a body to mourn, and to excrete the digested remains as waste?

The first example is an act of love, honour and dignity, the second is one of hatred, revenge and revelry in savage bestial butchery. Both are at the core of what it is to be human, and the distinction is a relatively minor one.

Love and hate, honour and butchery. You can decide for yourself what category provides the best fit for the actions of one who dines with and on his carefully chosen companions, treating their delicate meat as if it were the finest premium cuts of chateaubriand.

This time I made the choice not to leave the girl to the attentions of carrion birds, insects and beasts, I could not bear the waste. So instead I chose to share her with strangers, to fuse her component parts back with the living so that she could continue her existence. I had to work fast, but you will now find her in exquisite meat parcels on the shelves of Rugby's largest supermarket store, unless of course our ravenous brethren have consumed her completely already...

I finished the letter and felt ripples of shock running through my body. I felt like I had been wired up to some kind of low level electrical current, and my surroundings now seemed somehow less real. The original letter was with the document examiners down in forensics, but Lee had copied down the content word for word, allowing me and those others present - Big John Dodds and Sarah Theaker from CSI – to read the full extent of the horror for ourselves. Lee had told me that it had somehow found its way into his tray, and that he'd opened it absent mindedly without seeing that it was addressed to me like all of the others. He assured me that the revelations had been kept entirely to himself, so even unhappy as I was I let his actions go unquestioned for the time being.

'Just because he wrote it doesn't mean that it's true. It's no secret that most psychopaths are pathological liars.'

John Dodds spoke up first, shifting his massive frame uncomfortably in the restrictive plastic seat, ever the voice of reason and rationality even in the face of sheer insanity. He rested his gaze on me with calm solemnity, waiting for me to offer up my own opinion. His colleague watched us both, glancing from one face to the other and back again rapidly.

144

'You're right John, but if what he's saying is for real and we don't act on it right away then can you imagine the possible implications?' I said.

Silence reigned for long sobering moments while we all imagined the media shit storm and full scale public outrage. There would be lawsuits and widespread criticism, and that was just for starters.

Lee still looked as queasy as he'd sounded on the phone, and I couldn't say that I blamed him. I wasn't feeling too clever myself. There could be an unknown number of members of the public tucking into parcels full of human flesh for dinner while we sat here playing politics and debating our options.

'We tell the supermarkets immediately. Not necessarily about the nature of what we're facing, but enough so they pull every meat pie off their shelves until we get to analyse any that seem suspect. We can't risk just telling the biggest store and finding out later that he made a mistake on the size of the store.'

John suddenly burst out laughing and we all jumped. Sarah's mouth dropped open in amazement.

'I'm sorry everyone, but my wife just dropped me a text to ask what time I'll be home for tea tonight. She's just been shopping and she's making meat pie and mash with an interesting and unusual looking meat that she picked up from the supermarket.'

Chapter 47

Ian Barratt was the General Manager for the warehouse sized supermarket in central Rugby and he was definitely not amused with our request that he remove a whole section of valuable stock from his stores shelves. He kept us both standing up in his cramped office overlooking the shop floor, but to be fair, we'd have had to share a seat even if we'd been invited to sit anyway. Lee was persisting in being uncharacteristically quiet and still, seemingly happy to defer to me while he attempted to compose himself and his thoughts.

'So are you telling me or just asking me to comply with this strange and vague request?'

His green eyes flashed with petulance behind his designer glasses and he couldn't seem to leave his tie alone as he talked to me. The nervous activity made him look even younger than the mid to late twenties that I'd initially guessed at, like a teenager who'd borrowed his dad's suit for a job interview and found that it didn't quite fit comfortably.

'I have no legal power to force you to do what I'm asking yet, I'd need a court order to do that, but I'm having to act very quickly on information that's been received about that particular product in this specific store. Since I'm currently the most senior operational detective in the Warwickshire force, then I'm sure you'll appreciate that I've bypassed the usual formal channels for very good reason, and that this is not a minor offence that I'm investigating.'

I was getting irritated too, and I wanted to plant the seed that there might be something dangerous in the pies in his tiny mind. I couldn't understand the resistance in the first place. It wasn't as if we made this kind of request every other week, so even an utter moron should have been able to compute that we'd come here directly out of urgency.

'This is going to cost me money, and that's if I do decide to do it in the first place. That frankly isn't looking like a foregone conclusion in the absence of any kind of attempt at an explanation from you, by the way.'

He moved his hands away from his tie and started fussing with his over-gelled red hair instead. Seemingly, he was still labouring under the misapprehension that he was calling the shots on this one.

'I assure you that you would grow to strongly regret not going with my polite but firm insistence on this, and I promise you that if you do decide to ignore me then it will ultimately turn out very, very badly for you indeed when it all comes out, Mr Barratt.'

I was running out of ways to apply sufficient pressure on the officious little jobs worth, without outright telling him what was going on. I watched him take offence immediately, growing steadily more pink from the neck up to the ears as my vehemence riled him even more.

'I believe your thinly veiled threats have just made up my mind for me, Chief Inspector.'

He smiled nastily and then carried on.

'As you've already told me, I don't have to do anything that you say about this at the moment, and your refusal to give me a valid reason as to why I should leaves me entirely blameless in the event that my refusal proves to be the wrong decision. So if you don't mind, I'd like you and your colleague to leave now so I can get back on with my work.'

I looked across at Lee who was still away with the fairies by the looks of it, and then back at Ian Barratt who looked like he'd just scored the biggest win of his life, and the red mist well and truly descended over me.

'Then let me enlighten you on a couple of things you fucking idiot.'

He flinched at the insult and his hands went back to his tie for comfort.

'A young woman went missing a matter of less than two days ago, and so far we've been unable to find her. Fortunately we received some helpful information from the person purporting to have killed her, and we now have good reason to believe that pieces of her body are being rung through your tills in nicely packaged meat bundles, while we waste time up here debating about the best way not to inconvenience you and your precious little profit margin.'

Chapter 48

It had been necessary to give the store manager a stern warning about the implications if he was to repeat any of the strictly confidential information that he was now privy to, but since my tirade there'd been nothing but unswerving compliance with every single request that I'd made. CCTV footage spanning the time between Elizabeth's disappearance and receipt of the letter was obtained, and a team of junior detectives were tasked with watching the hours of footage in the hope of catching our man placing his substitute goods on the shelf. A number of suspect items had already been removed for analysis, the packaging on them being the same in most respects as the stores own brand products, but an annotated label underneath bore the word 'longpig'.

'Why longpig?'

I asked Lee, not understanding the reference and handing over another package to the forensic examiners.

'It's a word supposedly used to describe human meat in Polynesia apparently,' came the reply, making me look up at him in surprise.

'I just Googled it on my phone before you ask. I'm a little rusty on the finer details of cannibalism these days.'

He grinned but the gesture didn't reach his eyes, and he was still obviously deeply effected by the thought that a teenage girl had been processed like a slaughterhouse cow.

'Let's take five and get ourselves some fresh air, they can finish up in here without us.'

I began to manoeuvre Lee out of a door at the rear of the storage area, ignoring his weak protestations.

'I'm okay, Zara, just tired and frustrated.'

I ignored him until we were back out in the sunshine and fresh air.

'Let's get something straight, Lee, you're definitely not okay at the moment, but that's not a problem. This is beyond the pale and it's got us all rattled.'

I kept my hands on his shoulders, facing him as I spoke.

'Yes... sorry.'

He looked past me and I saw the fine creases in the corners of his eyes that he was too young to worry about yet, but which would grow steadily deeper as the stresses and strains of our work began to press down on him. Lee had spent almost three years in CID, compared to my eight, but the demands affect us all differently. Already I was seeing signs of burnout and was having to consider some respite for him.

'I'll keep this between us for now, but if I think for a minute that this is getting too much for you then I'll have you rested.'

His eyes flicked back towards mine, and there was unmistakeable hurt written in his expression. I'd seldom had cause to talk to him in this fashion, and never since we'd become intimate. I had hoped that he'd be able to see that I was acting out of concern for him, but his recognition of that fact seemed to be temporarily obscured by his upset.

'I've been on this case as long as you've been on it, and nobody has clocked up more hours and given more to trying to find this sicko than me. Don't you dare threaten to take that away from me out of some misguided sense of protectiveness, Ma'am.'

He shrugged my hands off and strode purposefully away from me towards the High Street, not looking back to see if I was following. Sharp little tears nipped at the corners of my eyes as I watched him go, feeling the sting of his switch to the impersonal use of 'Ma'am' like a slap.

I hoped that with a little time he'd come back with a sheepish apology, but I feared that he might not. I didn't want to lose him after everything else that had happened, but his rigid posture was so full of anger that I knew I'd just touched a nerve that might change things between us permanently. Remember the golden rule with men, Wade? Never injure their pride or they'll hold a grudge forever. The more I silently rebuked myself and tried to empathise with his position, the more I realised how it would have looked to Lee. I'd just pulled rank on him over a simple display of human emotion, hardly a capital offence. Twisted words from one of the Grey Man's letters swam back into my mind. Did they tell you how much it would cost you when you started out? And for the first time in my career I stood removed from myself and wondered what I had become.

Chapter 49

I arrived alone at Hallie and Mike's house with flowers, a bottle of wine and an excuse. Tonight was the night of mine and Lee's invite to sample Hallie's cooking, something which we'd both been looking forward to since the evening of the dinner party at my house where everybody had hit things off so well. Unfortunately, Lee was refusing to answer my calls and texts since he'd stormed off outside the supermarket earlier, and I had no idea whether he'd turn up independent of me or not. The laughter and fun that we'd all had together last time around seemed impossibly distant, like a fading snapshot in a discarded photograph album, and I felt a miserable weight of loss settling down for an extended stay in the pit of my stomach.

Hallie answered the door at the third knock, looking chic and glamorous again in black trousers and a deep purple vest top with glittering jade green detailing, and she leaned her head out to make an exaggerated scan of the surroundings for some sign of Lee.

'I'm afraid Lee couldn't make it this evening, so it's just little old me.'

I attempted a relaxed smile but the tension in my face wouldn't allow it. Hallie knows me so well by now that she knew without me having to say what was wrong.

'Oh babes, come here.'

She wrapped her arms around me tightly and I stifled a sob.

'Stop or you're going to make me cry, and I don't even know if it's

152

going to resolve itself by morning anyway.'

She let go of me and led me inside, where the smell of something mouth-watering drifted through from the kitchen.

'Well whatever that is that I'm detecting, I'm feeling better already.'

I said, as Mike emerged with a glass of red wine and kissed me on the cheek.

'I'm glad that my presence has that kind of power over you, Zara, but I've told you before, not in front of Hallie.'

He gave us both a self-satisfied grin and I couldn't help but laugh.

'So what's cooking anyway? I'm detecting, something curry based maybe?'

I sniffed at the air and followed them both through to the lounge, sipping at my wine as I took a seat.

'Nope, not curry, a lamb shank stifado, which is a slow cooked Greek dish with tomatoes, herbs and spices in the sauce; one of Mike's specialities.'

Hallie shared a look with him and I envied their closeness for a moment. Settled couples seem to have a kind of telepathy, and Mike had known not to ask about Lee's absence solely from the expression on Hallie's face. I didn't feel inclined to turn the evening into a forum about my relationship issues though.

'I bought along my suspects list, together with approximate times and dates of the murders.'

I unfolded the crumpled sheets of paper and tried to smooth them flat on the coffee table as they both leaned in for a closer look.

'Now I'm not expecting most of the names to be familiar to you, but I wanted to scratch off some of the ones that you do know, starting with Mike's.'

They nodded in unison and Mike sat back waiting for questions.

'Can you give me some kind of strong alibi for any of the dates and times, Mike?'

He leaned back in to get another look at the sheets, brow furrowing in concentration.

'July the third we were at your parents all day weren't we Hal's?'

He asked, looking up at her.

'Yes, and we were away with the boys in Scotland on that April weekend too.'

I drew a thick black line through Mike's name and sipped at my wine again, ignoring my stomach as it growled for food.

'Okay, what about Lee that should be an easy one to get rid of. Shit, sorry...'

Mike realised too late his unfortunate choice of words as Hallies shot him a fierce glance.

'Don't worry about it Mike, you're right, so let me think...'

I sat back in silence running over each of the murders in turn, not needing to refer to the sheet of paper since they were indelibly etched into my mind. I'd been with Lee when several of the bodies had been discovered of course, but I dimly realised that I hadn't been with him at the actual time of any of the killings themselves.

'He wasn't with me when any of them took place, so until I can think of a way to ask him about his other movements he'll have to stay on the list.

Chapter 50

The evening at Hallie and Mike's was soon over, and I walked the half mile or so home along well lit streets with my belly contentedly full of tender lamb and slightly too much wine. The Stifado had come accompanied with a sweet potato mash and Greek style bowls of side salad, and together we'd managed to scrub another half a dozen names of my suspect list using Hallie's encyclopaedic knowledge of the lives of our former university friends. I was embarrassed to learn that while I was a virtual social leper, she had maintained casual online friendships with many of those that I had long since lost touch with. There'd been a small quiet moment of sadness as I learned that a shy and cerebral ex-boyfriend from back then had lost his long battle with a brain tumour at the beginning of the year.

The air outside was still warm with the residual heat of the sunny day, and the perfume of flowers in people's front gardens scented the night that was closing in all around me. I watched a large hawk moth cutting a lazy trail between the silhouettes of trees, feeling much calmer than I had earlier in the day, until the streaking outline of a bat ended the insects life mid flight and whisked the body away for consumption and I thought of the Grey Man again.

As I approached my own front door I could see the shadow of a man standing in the porch, and my heart rate doubled until I caught sight of blond hair and recognised the shape as being Lee. I sincerely hoped that he hadn't come to finish it with me or to read me the riot act about my actions outside the supermarket, and I scoured his stance for clues about his demeanour as I got up close.

'Hi.'

Not exactly a killer line, but I couldn't risk leaving us both in silence as I rummaged in my bag for keys.

'Hi back at you. I know it's getting late, but I was wondering if I could come in?'

He looked uncomfortable and sheepish, and I couldn't decide whether that was a good or a bad thing.

'Have you been waiting out here for long?'

I finally found my key and unlocked the door.

'Not as long as I deserve.'

I felt an inner glow at the glimmer of an apology beginning.

'Well then, in that case I might make you stand out here a bit longer.'

I offered up a small hopeful smile which he returned, and I gestured that he should come inside to join me.

'I'm sorry about earlier, I know you weren't questioning my ability to do my job, but I couldn't get the image out of my head of him cheerfully making pastry and stuffing minced up dead girl in as a filling.'

He slipped off his shoes and hung his coat up on the rack in the hallway.

'That's okay. I didn't intend to get all official on you and start stamping my authority all over the situation. I was just worried about you, and your own health and well being comes first on this.'

157

I dropped my own coat down on the back of an armchair and headed for the fridge.

'I'm out of wine but I've still got a couple of cold Mexican beers left.'

I called back through to him, removing them from between plastic boxes full of salad and cold cuts.

'Cold beer always sounds good to me,' came back the reply, along with a sound like paper crumpling.

I stopped for a second, but the noise had finished, so I rooted around for a bottle opener and popped the caps off, leaving them where they landed on the kitchen worktop and debating whether to pour them out into glasses before deciding not to bother.

As I came back into the lounge Lee was nowhere to be seen, and I assumed that he'd nipped to the toilet until I heard the front door slam and footsteps moving quickly back down the short driveway. Confused I went to the window and separateD the slats of the blind with my hand, seeing Lee getting into his car and then pulling away at speed. My first assumption was that something else had happened on the case, but if that was it then surely he would have told me as my presence would have been required too? Then I saw the crumpled sheets of paper with my handwriting on discarded untidily on the seat cushion of the settee. My suspect list with his name on the bottom and a question mark alongside, and finally I understood.

Chapter 51

Grandma Madeleine left the girls to have fun in the playroom that she'd had carefully decorated like the one that still carried such fond memories from her own childhood, and quietly crossed over to the study, shutting the door behind her. She was not concerned about her husband arriving home and catching her, since they lived far enough out in the countryside that the sound of his car would tell her that he was home in plenty of time for her to cover her tracks if needed. Besides that, he was so accustomed to his comings and goings remaining unquestioned over the years that he wouldn't go looking for signs that she was checking up on him.

She logged onto the computer first and checked the search history, which was predictably blank, before systematically opening up each file that she could find and then closing it down again after she'd had a read of the contents. She didn't know what she was expecting to come across on the laptop, and her instincts told her that he was too careful to go perusing anything that might cause alarm, but she knew him well enough that even an item of vague curiosity would give her something to go on.

She had taken down a note of the timings of his 'business trips' over the last twelve months, including snippets about where he had stated or implied that he was going to on the infrequent occasions that he'd offered up any kind of clue, and now she intended to see how much of that was true if possible. She had even considered phoning up his workplace before, or checking his credit card statements, but the first action would no doubt have been reported back to him, and the second had proven impossible since he received his statements electronically to an email account that she didn't even know the address for, much less the password.

Closing down the computer, she stood and walked over to the imposing oak bookcase that stood next to a floor to ceiling window, stopping briefly to take in the view out over rolling hills and fields that stretched to the horizon. There were drawers in the unit, but upon trying to open them she found that they were both locked, and she stood on tiptoes to run her fingers across the top of the unit and then underneath the edge of the desk in a futile attempt to locate the keys. She paused again, breathing more deeply from her modest exertions and glanced up at the horrible painting that hung on the wall above his desk chair as she left the room.

The picture was a print of Francisco Goya's Saturn Devouring His Son, a bulging eyed giant figure with wild grey hair and a mouth stretched wide open as it went to take another bite out of the partially eaten white corpse clutched in its hands. It was an image from your worst nightmares, and its presence kept the girls out of this space. She had asked him to take it down on more than one occasion, but he had insisted that it stayed, citing the presence of artwork from such a master of the form as being a source of inspiration in his work. To her it was ugly and terrifying, the work of a man descending into madness.

The television was playing to itself as she moved back through into the sitting room and the news was on. Another report on the serial murder case that had been holding this part of the country in its grip for months was on. She'd had her fill of the new revelations that emerged almost daily, so she reached for the remote to switch over the channel.

'There is speculation rife that the so called Grey Man has struck again in the case of missing teenager Elizabeth Perry. The police have made no official acknowledgment at this stage, but we're getting unconfirmed reports that detectives visited this supermarket in central Coventry and took away items.'

The Grey Man. She registered the nickname and this time the painting immediately jumped back into her thoughts, joined by a sick light-headed feeling that set her off trembling.

She quickly walked back through to the study and went straight to it, lifting it away from the wall and seeing a small key taped to the rear of the canvas. Whatever was in those drawers she was about to see for herself now.

Chapter 52

In the cool of dawn I ran along a narrow dirt trail bordered by high thorny hedges filled with nervously flitting small birds, narrowing my eyes against the clouds of dust and grit that were being whipped up by the wind. I was pushing the pace hard, harder than I perhaps should have been doing, punishing myself and feeling the growing burn in my lungs at the sustained effort. My mp3 was playing a pre-selected track list that I'd named 'Angry Music', and harsh invective from Rage Against The Machine's 'Killing In The Name' was blasting into my ears to keep me company. I was concentrating hard on my discomfort, riding the waves of the feeling, and doing my damnedest not to think about what it would be like when I arrived in the office later that day.

The trail turned a sweeping corner and suddenly the wind was directly in my face, choking me with debris and sandblasting my exposed skin simultaneously, forcing me to slow down and turn my head over to one side. I spat chalky dust into the hedge bottom, coughing fiercely to clear my lungs but refusing to stop. Today I was in the mood for a fight and it didn't matter whether that was with Lee, the elements, or the Grey Man himself. In fact, if he knew what was good for him the Grey Man would take the day off.

When I came to a fork in the trail I took the turning away into the woods, abandoning the dirt track in favour of the less vicious attentions of occasional flurries of wind agitated leaves, knowing from experience that this route eventually rejoined the other one back down at the back of gardens on the housing estate. There are any number of different routes towards the same objective if you know the goal that you're aiming for well enough, Wade.

Rage Against The Machine gave way to Nirvana's 'Tourette's' as the path began to slope mercifully back downwards, and at last I was able to start catching my breath properly again. I wondered idly what different routes were at my disposal in tracking down the Grey Man, ignoring the seemingly remote possibility that he might be caught in the act of snatching a victim, using the mental exercise as a distraction from the growing physical pain in my legs.

There was my suspects list, but I was already starting to lose faith in that after last night, and a new profile was being discreetly prepared by Alan Hardwick's replacement. A new official list had been drawn up off the back of Elizabeth Perry's active secret second life, too. She had been living another reality underneath everybody's radar, and I had colleagues assigned to speaking with a diverse list of casual one time only lovers. My instructions were that the information was to be kept strictly to ourselves, as it could damage public sympathy for her if we decided to make an appeal, and that in turn would prevent some people from coming forward.

I remembered that Lee had taken on the task of looking into the deceased Doctor's odd assessment of who we should be looking for, but he'd been notably quiet on any progress that he'd made. Was it reluctance, or merely an acknowledgement of how busy I'd kept him on chasing up other potential leads; and if it was reluctance, what possible interpretations were there of that?

I dwelt on what a close analysis of the Doctor's movements and computer history might give me, and made a mental note to follow them up for myself with things lying how they currently did between me and Lee. The seed of the idea had been more of a hunch than anything else, but I'd had hunches proven right in the past and there could be no loose ends on this. I blanched at the thought that I'd only prepared half of an outline profile myself so far. Lee wasn't the only one who was being dragged in all different kinds of directions at once, or who was shirking his responsibilities. Thank you very much for that one, Emily. I thought, feeling horrible for blaming her at the same time.

I rounded the final long arc in the woodland track, seeing a small rabbit fleeing from me into the tangle of ivy and bracken with white flashes of its tail advertising its progress and alerting any of its friends to the danger. I knew that I needed my friends back on board if this was going to have anything like justice at the end of it too. That meant biting the bullet and explaining my actions to Lee sooner rather than later. There wasn't time for us to let our personal relationship get in the way with more young lives at stake.

Chapter 53

After the clean up the Grey Man stayed in remote cottage for another forty eight hours, seized by a cycle of alternately sleeping and then waking back up to eat. His waking state bordered on frenzy. He was initially exhausted with the effort that had been required in killing, butchering and processing the girl's body. But once he had regained some of his strength, he disposed of almost all of what was left over in the woods and then made arrangements to swiftly get his packages onto supermarket shelves.

For himself, he retained only certain select portions of her meat, together with Elizabeth's head, which he had placed on the dressing table by his bed while he rested. He had no fear at all of being discovered, and he was no longer troubled by nightmares and flashbacks about his actions in the way that he had been as a younger man, and so it was that he slept the deep, dreamless, sleep of the truly tired.

When the last of her flesh had been cooked and eaten, and the tiled room housing his mincing machine and associated tools had been comprehensively hosed down and then freshly repainted, it was time to think about going back home again. He contemplated the logistics of retaining her head for longer, even in death and without her body it still retained a certain beauty, but eventually ruled out the idea with deep regret.

'I only wish I could bring you back to life and do it all over again, Elizabeth. You were perfection.'

He lifted the head up by its long dark hair, wearing gloves now, and dropped it into a hessian sack that had been previously used to store potatoes in the outhouse, before placing that bag inside a larger plastic sack, twisting the top shut to prevent any spillage of fluids while it was in transit. He had special plans for where the bag and its contents were going to end up.

He manoeuvred the car out from where he had moved it under the shade of trees at the rear of the cottage and put the bagged up head in the boot, climbing into the driver's seat and setting off back into town. While it might not have looked like it, the cottage was on private property and remained unvisited by anybody except himself, and selected guests like Elizabeth, for ten months of the year. The other two months he let family stay for short breaks, but he always had large amounts of time in between in which to put everything back as it should have been.

On a whim he took a different route back around the town, intending to approach Coventry from the North of the city since he had no particular desire to sit in traffic all the way back. However, he realised it had been a mistake when he found himself queuing along a road that was usually pretty clear. He craned his neck out of the window as they crept along at walking pace for a few dozen yards at a time before stopping again, but couldn't initially see what the cause of the holdup was. More vehicles joined the slow procession behind the Jaguar, preventing him from easily changing his mind and turning the car back to take another route. The narrow lane would have been tricky enough to negotiate a turn in even without the additional obstacles.

He stretched out again as they queued around a bend and finally caught the reason for their slow progress. A solitary police car with its blue lights flashing was partially blocking the access. Stopping each of the cars to take a look in the back and then inside the boot. This was either related to the missing girl or to some other unrelated crime, but whatever the truth it was extremely bad luck. Even the fresh faced young constable up ahead was unlikely to miss a severed head in a bag, and trying to turn around now would draw attention to himself and risk some kind of police chase. In his favour was that the number plates on his car were registered to a fictitious company. He'd taken to swapping them as a precaution if the vehicle was ever spotted near to one of his tableaus or the scene of a disappearance. He opened the dashboard seeking inspiration, and what he saw inside gave him the seed of a plan.

Chapter 54

Lee wasn't in the office when I arrived which was highly unusual for him. at times when we'd first met I'd entertained the suspicion that he was living in the station since he always seemed to beat me here. I said a quick hello to one of the other detectives working under me, an intense and highly intelligent Asian girl called Geeta Badal, and received a tired smile and a nod in return. Geeta had entered the force on an accelerated graduate scheme several years previous and quickly demonstrated her value through a precocious aptitude for solving cases.

I wasn't quite sure where to begin without Lee's presence. I'd been intending to sit him down first thing for a frank discussion before getting stuck into further enquiries, as I hadn't wanted to get sidetracked and look as if I was either ignoring him or unconcerned by his prompt disappearance from my life. I headed for the canteen on the top floor and fixed myself a strong coffee to kill a little time, deciding that should give him enough scope to slope in late if he was stuck in traffic.

My phone began to vibrate in my trouser pocket as I was adding milk to the cup and I took my drink back down to my computer before I checked the message.

I put in for, and was granted immediate leave ahead of my request to transfer to Birmingham CID as soon as possible. I wish you a speedy resolution to the current case. Please don't call me. Lee.

The text message was grammatically precise and straight to the point, Lee Mead all over, and I was forced to adopt a casual attitude under the watchful gaze of Geeta and another junior colleague who'd just taken a seat at the desk opposite my own, even though my mind was spiralling.

It can't be true. He wouldn't just walk out on a case that has been his world for months on end, that's gotten right under his skin, without seeing it through to the end. Would he?

There was a stabbing pain of rejection in my chest, and I felt like I was going to be sick as I read the text over and over again, looking for some sign that it wasn't as I had first interpreted it.

'Ma'am. Are you okay?'

Geeta shifted uncomfortably as she hesitantly asked the question, peering at me over square framed glasses as she spoke. I knew that while she was incredibly effective, she was much more at home with facts and figures than with the emotional spectrum, and I'd had to deploy her with that in mind on the cases that she'd been assigned to in the past.

'Yes... sorry, I've just had news that we're losing a man from our team and the timing couldn't be worse to be honest with you. It's DS Mead, he's put in for a transfer to Birmingham and it appears that the request has been granted without the needs of our own ongoing investigation being taken into consideration.'

I forced a breezy business-like tone into my reply to mask the cover up the sound of my heart breaking inside me.

'I'm sorry to hear that Ma'am, but I'm very much at your disposal for any further support that's needed, if you can't change his mind.'

She measured out the words carefully and at that moment I knew that she was hungry for the opportunity, but that she'd also somehow been aware of the nature of mine and Lee's personal relationship too.

'Thank you, Geeta. I appreciate that.'

I let her know that she hadn't crossed a line with a small smile of acknowledgment, and she smiled in return, gathering up some paperwork off the printer and walking towards the door. As she went I suddenly realised that I could use her eagerness to save me some time and free me up to at least try to get through to Lee.

'In fact, Geeta?'

I caught the desperation in my voice and cleared my throat loudly.

'Ma'am?'

She stopped in the doorway looking back over her shoulder at me.

'There's an assignment that I'd asked DS Mead to work on but which he hadn't yet got round to. It's not hugely exciting, but I'm hoping that it might yield some important information for the case.'

Chapter 55

The Grey Man sat captive in his silver car and waited for his turn to reach the young police constable and submit to a search of his own vehicle. The detached girls head in the boot began to assume a heavy presence in his mind, and he could picture it rolling around to face in his direction, watching with interest to see how events might unfold. He had not come remotely close to being caught in possession of incriminating evidence for many, many years, and that was in no small part down to the extreme caution that he usually exercised in the aftermath of a killing. His current recklessness born out of a newly acquired level of supreme arrogance was uncharacteristic, and he silently cursed himself for making a mistake, vowing not to do so again once this next part was over with.

He realised with a start that the car in front had moved on again, leaving a sizeable gap between the two vehicles and prompting the driver behind him to hit their horn. The young officer was only five cars ahead of him now, and he looked up at the sudden noise before speaking a few words to the driver of the car that he'd stopped and beginning to make his way over towards the source of the disturbance. The Grey Man felt the tension creeping into his fatigued muscles, and a solitary bead of sweat rolled from underneath his arm down inside his shirt. he found himself holding his breath as the uniformed figure drew level with the silver Jaguar.

The policeman passed straight by and knocked on the window of the car behind that had sounded its horn, and the killer released the air from his lungs in a long steady stream, loosening his tight grip on the thin bladed knife that he kept in the glove compartment for emergencies. His tension had nothing to do with the prospect of having to kill the man when he asked to search the Jaguar's boot, and everything to do with knowing that he'd have to do so in front of multiple witnesses without anybody suspecting what was happening.

Having weighed up his scant options he'd settled on pulling his car close up to the police vehicle and around on enough of an angle to conceal his actions from the queue behind. That would allow him to drive the blade up into the cop's heart underneath the breastbone without being seen, although he'd have to open the car door in order to accomplish this feat unimpeded and risk doing so from a sitting position. If he pushed the cop away hard enough with his foot, then there was a good chance that he'd end up in the shallow overgrown trough at the roadside, and that would conceal him for precious seconds before the driver behind saw the dying man and came to his aid. He'd have to rely on a modest slice of luck in respect of nobody remembering the details of the false registration plate or a physical description for him, of course, but nobody would have reason to commit those details to memory until after the event and eye witnesses were notoriously bad at remembering such minutiae.

The officer finished rebuking the woman in the blue Citroen behind him and took a slow stroll back to his position at the roadside, waving in the next in line and making a quick cursory search of the interior as with the others. Me next. The Grey Man watched the car pull away with a cheery wave from the policeman to the occupants, and he rolled slowly up into position, concealing the knife beneath one of his thighs and opening up the driver's door.

'That's what I like to see, saving my legs and pulling up close.'

The younger man smiled, speaking confidently in a thick Birmingham accent, smoothing back his dark hair.

'Control to Charlie Tango four three, over.'

The crackle of a police radio drew the cop back over to his car before he was in range for the blade.

'Excuse me for just a moment please sir. Yes, go ahead control.'

He lifted out a handset and spoke into the receiver.

'Officer in need of assistance on Aldermans Green Industrial Estate, can you travel?'

The young man hesitated and looked back at the outwardly calm older gentleman in his expensive looking car. He didn't look like a monster.

'Yes, travelling now. I'll be there in less than ten minutes.'

He ended the transmission and smiled at the older man again.

'It seems that you're getting away with it this time,' he remarked with a smile. and climbed back into the police car, pulling away with tires spinning and the siren beginning a long mournful wail.

Chapter 56

I arrived back in the CID office late in the afternoon, slightly sweaty from a frustrating day of unsuccessfully attempting to track down Lee. I'd called, texted and even emailed him in a vain attempt to elicit some kind of response, explaining that I understood how hurt and betrayed he must be feeling, and that I wouldn't try to stop him from leaving for Birmingham if that was what he truly wanted, but that we needed to at least make some time to talk first. Nothing worked though, and it all remained resolutely silent from his end. Visiting his home had been no more successful, it was obvious that nobody was in and his car wasn't in its usual parking space. I scoured my brain for a better idea of where he might go when he was this upset with me, but got no further than 'anywhere that I wasn't likely to find him.'

The office was empty, but that wasn't at all unusual in the middle of a shift. much of the unglamorous legwork such as knocking on doors and speaking with witnesses was better off conducted in daylight hours, and it was necessary to get outside every once in a while to avoid going stir-crazy. I logged onto a computer and accessed my emails, quickly scanning through briefing reports about the mad, bad and dangerous who had finished serving time at Her Majesties Pleasure and were now back on the streets free to inflict mayhem again.

Further down the list I found one from Geeta, a terse one line introduction to the content accompanied by attachments detailing cases that Doctor Alan Hardwick had asked for the files on since he'd come onboard with the Grey Man case. The list was impressive, with details having been obtained about dates, times and locations of access to each of the files in case that was significant, although I hadn't specifically asked for it. Lacking in one or two interpersonal skills she might be, but Detective Constable Badal was thorough and she thought about why she was accessing information for an enquiry not just what the request had been.

I printed up a copy of the list and used my greater access rights to look back over some of the cases for any possible patterns. The biggest difficulty would come from identifying which ones he had been reviewing in relation to the Grey Man case, and which ones were unrelated and used for others that he had been working on simultaneously. Doctor Hardwick and his big reputation had been very much in demand by various other surrounding police forces. Another issue was going to be in determining which cases were for frame of reference. It was not especially uncommon for a profiler to review other previous crimes not necessarily linked to the same serial offender in order to check that his assumptions held up to closer scrutiny. I didn't have the luxury of assuming that any of the files that he'd accessed that weren't on our known list of connected offences had been reviewed because the Doctor had believed that they were committed by the same man.

I sighed and attempted to shift a stubborn curl away from my line of sight, but it sprang back each time I released my hold on it and I eventually gave up. The majority of the files that he'd accessed were old murder cases, with lurid images and descriptions depicting the handiwork of sexual sadists who were now safely behind bars. It was difficult to be certain whether he'd seen commonalities with the Grey Man series on many of them, but a handful included murders where the victim had been bitten, and one was an unsolved case where it appeared that the killer had drained off some of the dead girls blood into a glass and drank it.

I stopped reading and looked back at Geeta's list, ignoring the finer detail and trying to get an overview of the pattern of Hardwick's behaviour. Most of his work had been done from police computers, for which he had certain access rights courtesy of his long successful history in assisting on major enquiries, but there were half a dozen that had been accessed from his home office late at night and that were not existing murders in the Grey Man chain. I opened them up one after the other, quickly scanning the headline detail. All of them were from miles away, mainly in and around Plymouth in fact, and all of them were unsolved murders of young women. I frowned, to my knowledge the Doctor had never worked for a force that far South, although I'd get Geeta to cross check, but it was unlikely that unsolved cases would yield much of use for drawing up a profile since there was no known offender to draw comparisons to. I felt a tingle of something like anticipation, there was no reason to believe that these were significant yet, but they were the first incongruous information that I'd found and that had to count for something.

Chapter 57

When I arrived back at Coventry hospital in the evening at the tail end of visiting hours I found my way into the A Ward, where Emily was recuperating, barred. The stern nurse in grey who had given me directions on my previous visit was manning the desk and would not allow me to pass.

'I'm sorry, but it's not going to be possible for you to visit Emily today.'

She spoke firmly and eyed me defensively, as if talking to a difficult child and expecting trouble now that they'd not got their own way.

'Why, what's happened? I'm family, her older sister in fact.' I explained, panicking and fearing the worst, not able to read anything in the nurse's cool expression.

'She's fine, but she's specifically requested that you not be permitted to visit her again and I have a duty to honour that, particularly while she's still so fragile.'

She looked at me as if I'd crawled out from under a stone and I wondered briefly what else had been said about my small part in her reasons for being here.

'But that's ridiculous! I was here the other day, you spoke to me yourself, and she was absolutely fine with me at that point!'

I was becoming agitated, realising that it would make no difference, but feeling aggrieved and badly treated. Who did this woman think she was judging me without being in possession of the facts?

'If you are not able to moderate your tone with me then I'm afraid I'll have to call for security, Miss...?'

She waited for me to fill her in on my name.

'It's Acting Detective Superintendent Wade, and calling for security won't be necessary.'

I watched with satisfaction as one of her eyebrows rose and fell again in recognition of my status as a police officer and at the seniority of my rank, then turned away, mind made up to visit Fred Russell for now instead.

The loud echo of my rapid footsteps as I stormed back down the corridor away from the rude nurse at the desk was like slow motion gunfire. I slowed my pace as I registered that fact and pushed my way through double doors, almost knocking drinks out of the hands of a man trying to come through them from the other side.

'I'm so sorry, I didn't see you there...'

My voice tailed away as I realised that the man was Emily's husband David, and he gave me a self-satisfied smirk that stuck in my head before pushing past me and continuing back towards her ward. I quickly realised now why I was no longer allowed in to see her and I felt faintly sick as I recalled her asking me not to let him know she was here. I couldn't begin to fathom how he'd found her unless she'd relented and sent a message out to him herself, but ultimately there was nothing I could do about it besides stew at the moment.

To all intents and purposes he'd not done anything directly wrong towards her to trigger this, at least not that she'd decided to tell me about. I'd already had my chance to make him pay by prosecuting when he'd forced his way into my house, and I'd blown it. Backtracking now would look odd, I wasn't some vulnerable little girl who didn't know that the law would protect her, I was a senior detective heading up a major enquiry, and uncomfortable questions would be asked about both my motives and Lee's actions if I went after him now. Lee would believe that I was trying to make his transfer impossible, and his career could then be in jeopardy.

I accepted the situation for what it was. Another giant bloody mess to join all of the others that had come crashing down around me at the moment, as I moved away towards Fred Russell's room. But I made a mental note to revisit David further down the line. He was, after all, still on my suspects list too, even if, like Lee, he didn't match the physical description that we'd been working from.

Chapter 58

Madeleine spread out the papers that she'd found in her husband's locked drawers across the dining table and waited for him to arrive home. He'd texted her just over an hour ago complaining about heavy traffic and indicated that he would soon be back. The girls were now being happily entertained by a series of Disney films and a large bowl of home-made caramel popcorn out of the way in one of the bedrooms. The delay gave her plenty of time to process what she had discovered and to consider her options about how she wanted to tackle this problem, but her thoughts were a whirlwind and she still couldn't settle on exactly what to do for the best.

Finally, when she was on her third cup of coffee and beginning to feel jittery with the effects of the caffeine, she heard the sound of the car approaching, gravel crunching underneath the weight of the wheels.

She didn't move even when he was in the hallway and calling out to announce his arrival, but he soon located her and took in the sight of his private papers laid out on display.

'I can explain, Madeleine.'

He didn't look angry at her intrusion and his first reaction was to start offering excuses, which was strange. She'd have bet money on a violent reaction. Perhaps the presence of their grandchildren elsewhere in the house gave him additional pause for thought?

''I'm listening.'

She sipped from her cup and kept her eyes locked on him,

scanning for signs that he might suddenly flip.

'They're for a project that I'm working on for a client. I had to ensure that they were locked away to preserve client confidentiality, and to avoid this.'

He gestured towards the contents of the table.

'Bullshit. We've been together for far too long for me to fall for that old line anymore, dear. Now try again with the truth this time.'

Her voice was harsh and unforgiving, he'd sworn after the last time never to do this again and she'd believed him when he'd begged on his knees with tears in his eyes and promised that he could change. The same expression of contrition was creeping into his eyes now, but she couldn't bring herself to feel sorry for him.

'Well? Are you going to make me tell you what I believe, or are you going to be big enough to just admit it?'

The first flare of rage passed over his expression, but he forced it back away.

'Go on, tell me what you believe.'

His reply was hoarse and he clenched his fists involuntarily at his sides staring directly at her.

'There's an assortment of paraphernalia in here detailing places you've been, things that you've bought and plans that you've made. Together they tell me that you're seeing other women again.'

She turned her face to one side, blinking back tears.

'Have you forgotten already how that ended before? Have you completely blanked the girl from your mind?'

She was growing scarlet with emotion, her voice becoming a

fierce whisper. She put down her cup and dabbed at her eyes with a piece of scrunched up tissue.

'No. I haven't,' he replied softly.

'Well I bloody well hope not, because I did things for you on that night that I would never have done for anybody else. Even knowing what you'd been doing with her I still helped. You swore to me on our children's lives that you wouldn't put yourself in that position again.'

She paused, remembering the image of the lifeless girl in their bathtub and her naked husband standing over the battered body. He'd been a young man then, barely out of his twenties, and she'd suspected that there were other women in his life but never expected to meet one like this. I didn't mean to. He'd said with wide fearful eyes, and, not knowing about the others, she'd believed him.

Chapter 59

Unable to contact him in any other way, I resorted to staking out Lee's house at night after my shift had finished. I borrowed one of Hallie and Mike's cars for the task after giving an awkward explanation, a nearly new smart black Volvo SUV, so he wouldn't recognise my own car and drive away immediately, and settled in for what might be a long wait feeling vaguely like a love struck teenager stalking her celebrity of choice. To pass the time I listened to Zane Lowe's show on Radio One, enjoying the enthusiasm and playful banter, and discovering a beautiful atmospheric new track by Clare Maguire called Ain't Nobody that held my attention rapt as it was played an unprecedented three times back to back.

'Ain't nobody can love me like you do...'

I   felt like the artist was singing the story of my current pain and turmoil directly to me, and I blinked away a tidal wave of self pity.

When the track finished its third time through I snapped back out of it and checked my phone for messages out of habit. Ignoring texts about compensation I might be entitled to and banks I could claim money back from, before I found one from a familiar number that made my heart begin to race.

'My car's in for a service and I'm watching you from the living room. I take it you're not going to sit out their all night? Lee.'

I looked back up at the property, which was still in darkness despite the fact that night had well and truly fallen, feeling utterly self conscious and wondering how long he'd been aware of my presence. A stab of pure anger at being left sitting here followed hot on the heels of the awkwardness, and I had to take a couple of deep calming breaths before I got out of the car, reminding myself that I was here on a peace mission not for another fight.

It was colder than I remembered outside away from the comfort of the Volvo's efficient heater, and I fought the urge to shiver, keeping my posture upright and my expression neutral. I crossed the dark road feeling detached from myself, all of a sudden hyper-aware of every single aspect of my movements. The streetlights bathed everything in a supernatural yellow glow, and I looked up at the sudden noise of an approaching engine revving hard as I reached the pavement outside Lee's house. I found myself frowning and squinting but not able to see anything besides the single bright headlight of a motorbike, so I continued on my way and ignored the recklessness of speeding along a quiet residential road for now.

Lee spared me the indignity of knocking and waiting for an answer, opening the door before I got there. Not quite a big hug and an all is forgiven, let's go to bed, but a start at least, and for that I was embarrassingly grateful at this particular moment in time. He was unshaven and there were dark circles around his eyes. It looked like he'd been crying. I opened my mouth to speak, praying for something poignant and free from accusations or recriminations to come out, but the noise of the motorbike engine gave way to the sound of hard breaking, the screech of rubber on tarmac, forcing my attention back towards the road.

I didn't see the hessian sack arcing through the air until it struck me hard in the chest, the hard heavy item inside knocking me to the ground and winding me badly. But I caught sight of the salute from the leather-clad helmeted figure on the bike as he accelerated back away from the kerbside and rounded the corner. Lee was beside me almost instantly, all antagonism between us temporarily forgotten, helping me back up to a sitting position and urging me to lean forward while I gasped and tried to catch my breath.

'I think there's a brick or something inside the bag, my ribs are hurting really bad.'

I managed, wheezing as I began to recover, and seeing Lee lift it up and turn it over to empty out the contents.

It took a fraction longer than it should have done for me to recognise the item that fell out, and I covered my mouth with my hands in shock when I did. The bag contained a severed head that I assumed must have once belonged to Elizabeth Perry. But its hair had been cut, dyed and curled in a passable approximation of my own style.

Chapter 60

It felt surreal lying down on the comfy settee in Lee's neat minimalist living room with its familiar expanse of magnolia and cream colours, now that the head had been recovered as evidence and we'd both agreed to have statements submitted by mid-morning. I couldn't help noting that there were still no signs of photographs and other personal items to advertise that a real human being lived here. I'd lost count of the number of occasions on which I'd teased him about his decorative choices, and they hadn't made one jot of difference anyway. Lee was happy with the canvas blank for now.

'Here, drink this, and for the record, I still think you should get checked out at the hospital.'

He handed me a good measure of malt whisky in a small tumbler and I sat up painfully to accept it from him.

'Thanks.'

I took a sip and swallowed it straight down, enjoying the warm glowing feeling that followed.

'I'm okay now though. It was just something of a surprise to get hit by a head that wasn't attached to somebody.'

I raised an eyebrow and he let the smile that he'd been holding back spread across his face.

'Still think I'm the killer?'

He delivered the question nonchalantly, but his smile faded back away and I saw the pain behind his eyes.

'I never thought you were the killer, not even for one second. I was just working on something crazy that I stupidly didn't share with you from the outset, and the result was relationship Armageddon when you stumbled across it.'

I shifted into a more upright position, wincing at the bruised feeling in my chest as I did so, but wanting him to see that I was sincere now that I had his attention.

'Think about it Lee. Even ignoring the obvious fact that you're not a frothing at the mouth psychopath with a deep seated hatred of women, you don't match the description or any of the profiles that we've worked from, good and bad. I trust you implicitly and I'd stake my career on you being straight down the line in every aspect of your life. That's just one of the reasons why I want you in mine.'

I took another sip of the smoky whisky and cast my eyes down to let him process what I was saying without scrutiny.

'I've had my transfer request accepted and the notice to my landlord on this place has been put in. He's already got plans to let it out to his niece…this is all coming too late.'

I watched him thinking about the logistics and the hassle of trying to undo what had been put into motion.

'You really hurt me, Za. And that was after you promised not to keep things from me about the investigation again. You don't do that to people that you trust and care about. At least not if you want to keep them close to you.'

His grey eyes rested on me solemnly, and for a moment he looked much older and sadder than his years should have allowed.

'I'm sorry.'

Simple words but I meant them with all of my heart.

'I know you are, but it doesn't change the fact that I'm now effectively homeless and jobless unless I follow through on the Birmingham move.'

He reached out for the bottle of scotch labelled Highland Park that was resting on a side table and topped up both of our glasses.

'The list you saw was me building on the theory that the Grey Man is close to me in some way, perhaps even closer than we've ever considered before. It started out as simply a list of offenders that I'd arrested in the past, but we both know how that panned out when it was looked at in the first place. So I extended it to include a much broader cross section of the men in my life, including people like you and Mike, even though you're obviously not involved in these offences. The intention was to quickly scrub your name back off as soon as it could be demonstrated that you couldn't possibly have been there, but I wanted to do that without coming out and questioning you because I didn't want to ruin things for us. Obviously that plan worked out spectacularly.'

I studiously avoided mentioning that I'd spoken to Mike and Hallie about the case over him for now. One revelation at a time seemed wiser.

'Okay. But I'm serious about the home and work situations, and they might not be possible to undo.'

He rubbed at his eyes with his thumb.

'I think I can sort out both of those things for you, Lee. I'll speak to Birmingham Central CID in the morning and iron it all out, and on the home front, you could always move in with me...'

Chapter 61

The Grey Man lay in bed beside his sleeping wife and watched mental images of his crimes playing out across the plain white ceiling above. For once he remained uncritical of his own performance, allowing the pictures to run like videos without analysing their content in detail, the sole occupant of a private and elaborate cinema straight out of hell. He was calm again, despite a tiresome and infuriatingly long evening of listening to Madeleine prattle on and on about a crime that was so long ago and so utterly unimportant to him now that he could barely summon up more than a couple of freeze frames of the girl. Even then they were almost devoid of colour and detail, her face and hair colour now lost in the recesses of his mind along with many others.

He sat up carefully, not wanting to find himself subject of further scrutiny, and paused to make sure she was genuinely asleep, satisfied when he saw no change in the rhythmic rising and falling of her chest. How easy it would be to place a pillow over her face now and keep it there until her struggling stopped.

He pushed aside the desire to kill her as he had on a countless number of occasions over the course of their life together, amusing himself with the thought that he was in all probability not alone in that respect. If it took an absence of emotion to accomplish the taking of multiple lives, then why were so many murders committed by people of the ones that they were supposed to love the most? He strongly believed that murder required a particular kind of passion, otherwise there would be no reasonable explanation for the overwhelming feelings that accompanied the commission of his crimes and that drove him to repeat those actions over and over again.

Killing Madeleine, who on some level was aware of the nature of what he was and what he was capable of, would be an acknowledgement that he was ready for this journey to come to an end. He had already decided long ago that he would carry on until the time came that he could look into the eyes of whatever had created him, if such a twisted being existed.

The desire to kill had been much stronger in him than he was accustomed to in recent times. He'd grown used to thinking of that part of himself as a vast black snake which required him to feed it to bursting every once in a while, but then coiled back up and lay sated and dormant. Gradually, as the years had passed, he'd become aware that the beasts appetite was growing quietly but insistently, and the spaces between 'feeds' had shrunk from years to a matter of mere months, which made the planning that much more difficult and imprecise. Now he realised that he'd killed three times in quick succession with barely a pause for breath in between. The Doctors death had been out of necessity, and one of the girls out of opportunity, to be sure, but the sense of inner quiet that should have descended after such an orgy of chaos and mutilation was notably absent.

He realised that he was out of bed and on the landing now, standing outside the guest room with the door ajar and the soft breathing of the two sleeping girls within clearly audible. The antique grandfather clock which lived at the top of the stairs, and that had been passed down from generation to generation, ticked slow tense seconds by, one hundred even rhythmic clicks before he turned with an effort of will and moved back away towards his own bedroom again. The dark and growing behemoth inside the man hissed in bad tempered discontent and settled into an unhappy and uneasy slumber, waiting for another chance to emerge.

Chapter 62

Lee's arrival back in the Coventry CID office was greeted with lukewarm enthusiasm, since one or two of his junior colleagues had already been assessing the progression opportunities that would be afforded by his absence. I'd already filled him in on Geeta Badal's valuable input in chasing up a loose end that we'd simply not had time for, and we were both in agreement that she was more than capable of handling some additional responsibility. As such, Lee's first task had been to speak with her privately about taking a more prominent position in the Grey Man enquiry, while also being mentored by himself for a step up to the rank of Sergeant at the earliest possible opportunity. Predictably she'd jumped at the chance, and we now had her cutting an ultra efficient swathe through the list of previous offenders arrested by myself over the course of my career, sifting out those that were dead, incarcerated or just plainly wrong for these offences for other clearly definable reasons.

With a large burden of work off our shoulders we were able to backtrack over the curious activities of Doctor Hardwick in the course of his final months of life. Of particular note was the cluster of unsolved murders around Plymouth, the oldest of which had occurred more than thirty years ago. They were interesting because Geeta had found no discernable reason why he would have needed to view these cases. Hardwick hadn't been working on cold cases, or on behalf of any other major enquiries which could feasibly tie in with those files while he was helping us with the Grey Man murders. So why on earth was he interested enough to quietly obtain and access them on multiple occasions?

'Theories?'

I asked for the tenth time that day.

'Well, they look like they're connected to each other, but they don't have any of the characteristics I'd associate with our guy, no cannibalism or staging, no letters to the police. The only discernable similarity is the fact that they're all youngish female victims. Maybe the Doctor had some theories about who was responsible for them and was running a completely unrelated project of his own. There'd be some serious kudos in solving a big cold case like that surely?'

Lee looked as confused as I felt while he gave voice to the thought that neither of us wanted to accept might be true. There had to be something in here that we were missing. Serial killers weren't exactly ten a penny in the UK like they appeared to be for our American and South African counterparts.

'Who did they think they were looking for at the time?'

I played with a loop of my hair and sighed, waiting for something to strike me and make sense of it all.

'There were various theories doing the rounds from what I can see, and probably another dozen that aren't in the file. But there weren't any reliable witnesses to the girls actually being taken, so just a vague physical description that could have been anybody, and nothing else concrete...Let's see...they spent time talking to naval officers at the base, seemingly because knots found on some of the rope used to tie up the victims were of a type used by the navy. Not much ocean near to hear though. There are your usual half-snippets of hearsay too, a working girl who reported the number plate of a punter who supposedly confessed to one of the murders, stuff like that.'

He stopped and looked up at me, checking whether he should carry on.

'Did they trace the punter?'

I was pacing around now, hoping that the movement would set the cogs in my head back into motion.

'No. She wasn't sure whether she'd mixed up the last few letters, and when they tried running both versions through the computer they came up with prominent persons who were too important to risk bothering, and too old to be their guy.'

He pulled an unhappy face and we shared a look of recognition. Connected to our offences or not, the officers on these cases hadn't exactly turned over every stone. Any officer on my team using status as a reason for not troubling somebody in a murder enquiry would have been back in uniform before they'd finished offering the excuse.

Chapter 63

When we'd done for the day Lee had finally relented and agreed to move in with me, but only for a short period of time until he could find himself somewhere suitable to rent alone again. I didn't argue with his assertions that we'd each still need our own space for a while yet, that we weren't ready for that level of commitment in our relationship on a permanent basis, since I was relieved that that he'd even agreed to stay at all. Truth be told, I knew that the difficulty I'd had in trusting him with aspects of my life and the investigation made it impossible to argue otherwise, but at least our new reopening of lines of communication had allowed me to definitively cross his name off my list of suspects once and for all.

I offered to help him start packing up boxes, but he politely declined and now I'd been left alone to return to an empty house, which seemed strange and disquieting after I'd been growing accustomed to both his and Emily's presence around the place in recent times. In an attempt to fill the silence I found myself switching on the television and the CD player to keep me company, as I prepared something to eat and ran back over the latest points of interest in the Grey Man case. The more I pondered the significance of the Plymouth murders, the more it seemed likely to me that Hardwick had reason to believe that they were the work of the same offender. The question was, what had he seen to connect such geographically disparate chains of offences that we were managing to miss? It was too big a stretch to put it down to pure dumb luck or simple chance, so that had to make it something relatively big, surely?

I combined single cream to a beaten egg and added it to a mixture of cooked spaghetti, bacon, garlic, and grated courgette, stirring it through and letting the residual heat from the pasta cook the liquid briefly before tipping it into a large bowl. Thank you for this one Emily, you taught me to make courgette carbonnara and in return I helped drive you to a suicide attempt and then back into the arms of your scumbag husband. What a rock I turned out to be for you.

I sat down on the settee, which still bore the faint orange scars of mine and my sister's fight, trying to recapture the feeling of personal triumph that had briefly surfaced in the kitchen as I quietly celebrated cooking a meal that didn't involve packets, tins or the use of a microwave. But the thought of Emily ruined my enjoyment of both the moment and the meal. Memories, a blessing and a curse. Wait. I stopped with my fork halfway up to my open mouth, tuning out the background noise from the TV and radio while I chased the tail end of a fast escaping thought. How had Hardwick connected two separate serial murder cases that were so far apart? It had to be because he had prior knowledge of the Plymouth crimes. Hardwick must have worked the profile or consulted on those cases at some point in the pass. Yes, now I thought about it, hadn't there been a distinct southern accent in there somewhere? Taking the theory one step further, had Hardwick somehow worked out who was responsible? Was that why he had to die?

I realised that the fork was still hovering in mid air in front of my face and put it back in the bowl, all traces of my appetite vanishing at the growing realisation that this was the beginning of the breakthrough that I so badly needed. If my hunch was right and Hardwick had indeed unravelled this puzzle, then all we needed to do was find the connection for ourselves and follow the trail to our killer.

The Grey Man was hiding somewhere in the fine detail of the Plymouth files, I'd stake my pension on it.

Chapter 64

The two girls, Lexie and Annabel, woke Grandma Madeleine with a start, greeting her with the sight and sound of clanking porcelain from the breakfast tray of toast, coffee and orange juice that they were carrying into the bedroom. She realised right away that her husband was gone, sliding her hand over to his side of the bed and feeling the cold that told her he'd been up for hours.

'We've been making famous chef's breakfast!' announced Lexie, handing over her side of the tray and urging the younger Annabel to do the same with an excited grin. Madeleine rubbed the grit out of the corners of her eyes as she sat up and stifled a yawn.

'Thank you very much, it's not every day that I get served my breakfast in bed, especially by famous people like yourselves.'

She replied, playing along with a quick wink and a tired smile and lifting a slice of lukewarm toast up to bite with exaggerated enjoyment for their benefit.

'Is it nice Grandma asked Lexie?' looking all of a sudden very serious.

'Yes it is. In fact it might just be the best breakfast I've ever had! Where's your Granddad got to anyway?'

She sipped some of the fresh orange juice and made the question seem casual.

'He's making pancakes for us in the kitchen. He says we can have our break now!'

They beamed in unison while she tried not advertise her surprise at what they were telling her. In over thirty years together she'd never known him to fix her breakfast. That was a woman's job he'd announce grandly, a fragment of outdated residue from his own upbringing, but one that she minded much less than some of the others.

'Could you bring this tray back downstairs between you for me so we can all eat at the breakfast table together, please?'

She handed the tray back over and got up, putting on a white towelling dressing gown quickly and following them back downstairs, urging them to take their time.

The sound of the radio blaring out from the kitchen reached her ears before she arrived at the foot of the stairs and her concern and confusion deepened immeasurably. The volume was up way too loud; playing the kind of music that he always referred to as 'inane crap' and refused to have on in a room that he was sitting in, and that was another first. The girls pushed on ahead before she could obey her instinct to stop them, bursting through the half open door singing 'Granddad, Granddad, Granddad' excitedly, and she hurried through after them.

The extractor fan was whirring, competing with the noise of the radio for attention, and a plate of scotch pancakes rested next to a pot of honey, one of chocolate spread and one of strawberry jam on the island unit that served as a breakfast bar along one side. Granddad himself was nowhere to be seen, and the door leading out to the gardens was left hanging wide open.

'Girls, you both sit down and make a start on these pancakes, I'm just going to track down Granddad to join us.'

She propelled them to their seats with gentle but insistent shoves, pasting a taut smile in place and scanning the view out of the window as she did so. Wherever he'd gone to it wasn't the garden, there was nowhere to hide for a person of his size on the open expanse of neatly manicured lawns and flowery borders, but apparently he wanted her to believe that he'd gone out that way. She closed the back door and turned the key in the lock, taking one last look back to make sure the children were okay before she set off to search through the each of the rooms in the rest of the house. He was in here somewhere or she'd have heard the car on the driveway.

Chapter 65

One in the afternoon, and I was eating a flaccid unsatisfying chicken salad sandwich at my desk in the CID office while Lee enjoyed a heavily vinegar saturated bag of chips with gravy and mushy peas opposite me. We were discussing my latest brainwave about Hardwick's interest in the Plymouth series in between mouthfuls, and I was trying hard not to launch myself over the desk and face first into Lee's lunch in preference to my own undoubtedly healthy but ultimately tasteless option.

Geeta Badal had swiftly established that the Doctor had been involved with those cases in a peripheral capacity, as it had turned out that he was something of a maverick and a rising star in the pioneering field of British forensic psychology at a facility nearby at the time. However, that still didn't explain why he'd made an automatic connection to the Grey Man series all these years later, and we were sounding out different similarities while we waited to stumble across something striking.

'What about the fact that restraints were used on all but one of the victims? I know that fact in itself isn't especially unusual, but what about the method and techniques? Is there anything that could constitute a signature?'

Lee tapped away at his keyboard for a few seconds, locating details of the bonds used in some of our cases. I watched him intently, smiling at his concentration face and trying unsuccessfully again to ignore his chips.

'The knots used on our victims aren't exactly the same as the ones before, but they're still nautical ones, like those used by sailors of all varieties, which is a link of sorts. What defines our murders would you say?'

He looked across at me expectantly and I took a bite of my sandwich to buy myself more thinking time before I answered.

'That they're very controlled and planned as a general rule, obsessively so in fact, and they revolve around food and dining. Sarah Jennison's leg was hacked off and roasted over hot coals, Charlotte Thomas had sections of her abdomen used for sushi rolls, Carla Tonelli's upper arm was pot roasted with seasonal vegetables...'

I pulled a disgusted face.

'I take it I don't need to go on?'

Lee shook his head slowly, frowning.

'And there's the letters to you with these ones. Where does that fit in?'

He was asking rhetorically, but I answered anyway.

'I'm not entirely sure, but since the first Plymouth murder was thirty years ago, I'll remind you that I'm not that old, Sergeant!'

He blushed and looked momentarily panicked.

Oh no, I wasn't...'

I cut him off and waved away his protestations.

'It's alright, I know you weren't meaning anything by it, and the question's definitely a valid one. The way I see it we just need to find the point at which these older crimes meet with a suspect who is somehow connected to me and that's where we'll find our man. So where do we go from here?'

I asked and stood up to lean across the desk, helping myself to a mushy pea covered chip and popping it into my mouth. In comparison to the chicken sandwich it tasted like heaven.

'Hey, get your own! Serves you right for settling for something you didn't actually want for lunch.'

He laughed and swatted away my attempt to net myself another chip.

'It's your fault for leading me towards temptation! You can't eat a bag of chips in the office without expecting to have to sacrifice a few to your colleagues, it's an unwritten byelaw!'

He relented and lifted up the tray so I could help myself to a few more, and I tossed the remains of my sandwich into the bin ten feet away with a practised flick of the wrist.

'Seriously though, looking at these as all belonging to the same series, with the older crimes as the key. What would you put at the top of your to do list?'

I gave a bow to an imaginary appreciative audience for my impressive sandwich throw.

'It's got to be those two vehicles that were never followed up, they're probably nothing but it should have been done anyway.'

I nodded my agreement and began logging a request for information from the DVLA database.

Chapter 66

'For somebody whose home was so outwardly minimalist you have a ridiculous amount of stuff!'

I huffed and wheezed as I carried heavy box number ten from the hired panel van through the hallway and upstairs into the spare bedroom, following Lee who was making much lighter work of his own load up ahead.

I'd let him choose whereabouts he wanted to put his things, and much of it was now destined to find a new temporary home in the loft. But the stuff that he wanted to keep out was ending up neatly stacked in the smallest bedroom. We hadn't yet discussed where he was planning to sleep tonight, and I was kind of hoping that if the day panned out as expected, it was going to be something which made itself apparent without the need for talk.

'You're the one who thought this would be a good idea in the first place, it's a bit late to decide that you don't like me bringing along my belongings now.'

He put down his box and grinned to let me know that there wasn't any malign intent in the comment, and reached out to take my box off me.

'My arms are killing me, I'm going to need a rest soon or I'll keel over.'

I wiped a line of moisture away from my hairline and leaned back against the bedroom wall.

'That's most of it now anyway. The odds and ends can wait until your delicate lady arms and legs have recovered a bit!'

He smirked in amusement.

'Careful mister or you'll be finding that new home elsewhere a lot faster than you thought!'

I cocked an eyebrow and tried to look fierce and serious, but failed miserably and collapsed into a fit of laughter.

'That's better, I've not seen you have a good laugh often enough recently,' he said, and placed my box down on top of some of the others.

'Which is a crying shame by the way.'

He took a step back towards me, smiling that self assured smile that had driven me to the very brink of distraction a dozen times a day from the very first moment we'd met, right up until the time when we'd inappropriately locked lips for the first time in the aftermath of securing the tough convictions of a gang of highly organised armed robbers.

I felt time slowing down. I could still close my eyes and revisit that exact moment in my mind. The surprising softness of his lips on mine in direct contrast to the roughness of his short stubble against my cheek, the strong masculine smell of Boss aftershave and the strange uncontrollable trembling that had taken up residence in my arms and legs.

'Oh, and why's that, Detective Sergeant?'

I asked in a low whisper that advertised my feelings about the current situation. I'd play hard to get another time.

'Because you are the most beautiful woman that I've ever seen,

Zara, and that effect is increased threefold when you laugh or smile.'

He stepped in again, and we were suddenly close enough for me to feel his warm breath and see his black pupils dilating in arousal and anticipation. I could feel the trembling that had gripped me the first time starting up again now as I closed the final space between our bodies and he stooped ever so slightly to bring his lips down to mine.

'The bedroom's only next door.'

I offered breathlessly, knowing full well that he'd been here often enough to be aware of that fact, but wanting him so much I was almost panting.

'We won't make it that far right now, Ma'am,' he replied and began to unbutton my shirt, as we started to kiss more urgently.

Chapter 67

I lay awake in the darkness, listening to the distant rumble of cars passing by on the main road with Lee's heavy arm resting comfortably across my stomach. He'd been asleep for hours it seemed, and after an afternoon of considerable exertions that weren't limited exclusively to moving and unpacking boxes, by rights I should have been too. Unfortunately, happy as I was with the first steps truly taken towards getting back on track with the most important relationship in my life, I couldn't get thoughts of the investigation to leave me alone for long enough to be able to drop off.

I thought about the crimes in Plymouth, five murders over the course of nine years that then stopped just as suddenly as they'd started when the killer moved on or changed his modus operandi and began to hide the bodies better. I knew from experience and from intensive courses that I'd attended that serial offenders tended to escalate, eventually so consumed by their twisted desires that they existed in perpetual frenzy until they were caught, or old age denied them the ability to continue to commit their unspeakable crimes. Our killer was getting older, but he was evidently not so decrepit that it had yet had an effect on his ability to murder and mutilate. Then there was the 'gap'.

I shifted around, trying to escape the gossamer threads of the investigative part of my brain, but the 'gap' kept coming back. It was impossible to escape the fact that there had been something like eighteen years between the final known Plymouth slaying, and the first in the Grey Man series. There was a strong possibility that somebody who'd been this careful and lucky had not wound up in prison during that time. If I was right, he'd remained free to kill whenever the mood took him for all of those years. Even if I didn't factor in the likelihood of his need to kill becoming more frequent over time, a point that flew in the face of what the current murders demonstrated, that meant there were at least another nine out there that we didn't know about, and probably very many more.

Did he maintain a respectable façade, veiled behind the mask of a normal family life?

I thought about the chaos left in the wake of the Gloucestershire serial killers Fred and Rosemary West, where there'd been a house full of children and frequent transient visitors, as well as neighbours and social services in close proximity, but seemingly nobody suspected that the two were a tag team of serial killing sexual sadists. There'd been a general acceptance that the number of murders in that series was significantly higher than had been uncovered, again because of a large gap in between killings. Serial killers don't take time off, they live for their crimes.

I dwelt on that case for a moment, despite the feelings of tension and disgust that it provoked in me. There'd been whisperings of cannibalism there too, it seemed to be a natural progression for a certain type of offender who inhabited the dark outer regions of human behaviour. Was that why we hadn't seen the link for ourselves yet? Had Hardwick seen the beginnings of something in those earlier cases that would incubate over time and then hatch out into this madness? If he had finally cracked both sets of cases why had he then kept that to himself? Why would any sane person put their own material needs ahead of the lives of innocent young girls?

I ran back over what I could remember having read about the historic murders in my head, trying to make them fit with signs of a growing desire to consume human flesh. Laura Nightingale, strangled and badly beaten, with her throat slit after death, Imogen Jenkins, strangled and beaten too, her throat slit and the tip of her tongue missing, presumed to have been bitten off by herself in the struggle and then eaten by rats that were all over the scene. What if the rats weren't to blame? What if Laura's throat was slit to drain away blood for consumption? I felt the certainty growing inside me and made a note to check on the others for other question marks in the morning. Most of all I prayed that our man did not have his own 'Rose' to share his passion for murder with, but if he did then I'd see her locked in the deepest darkest hole I could find as well.

Chapter 68

Night had fallen and still her husband had not turned up. Madeleine had reassured the girls that he'd had urgent business to attend to that had caused him to rush out. But they were starting to get towards an age when they realised that adults didn't always tell them the truth, and she could tell that Lexie in particular wasn't buying the explanation fully. She'd searched the house from by room after they'd found breakfast made and the back door swinging in the breeze, convinced that he was hiding from her after the tough talking that had been done the previous evening, but there'd been no sign of him. It seemed liked a stretch to believe that he'd simply walked or run out of the back door, scaled the fence and headed out into the open countryside, but that was the only reasonable supposition left. The worrying thing was that they were a relatively long way out from civilisation, and the nearest shops and houses were a three mile hike along one track country lanes. Anybody walking along those was risking their life since people drove along them like lunatics despite the high stone walls and abundance of tight turns.

She'd found herself being short with the older girl as she got her and her sister ready for bed, sick and tired of the constant questions that she couldn't quite answer, and trying to fend off her enquiries about when their parents would be coming back to fetch them. The short answer was that she didn't know at the moment. The phone calls from both parents had stopped a couple of days back, and when she'd tried calling their dad's mobile the line wouldn't connect and the number their mum had left as an emergency contact just rang out. The agreement had been that dad would pick them back up after a week, but that deadline had now long since come and gone.

She scoured her brain for ideas about where he might have gone to in his current state of mind, pushing aside the snapshot image of Lexie crying out in pain when she'd brushed her hair far too roughly in anger. Her husband might believe that his movements were a complete mystery to her, but she'd developed certain instincts about the boltholes he might use in a crisis, and her money was on the cottage that they supposedly retained for family use up in the hills.

As a younger man he'd shown her a stash of impressive looking knives and a pristine crossbow that he kept in a locked box up there, his face alight with an excitement that she'd seldom seen in a man who was usually almost monotone in his emotions. He'd been a keen hunter for years even at that point, and he'd often told her in moments of quiet reflection that the most valuable things his own father had taught him were how to kill cleanly and effectively, and how to butcher your kill. There'd been a period of time after he was discharged from the Navy when he'd travelled the world on hunting trips, and sometimes she'd accompanied him, although she never went out on the hunt herself, preferring to listen to his anecdotes afterwards and then chide him until he took a shower and washed the blood off his hands and face.

When he went without his trips for too long he became edgy and difficult, and that's when they'd hit one of their rocky patches and he'd even raised his fist to her on more than one occasion. She'd resolved that glitch by removing the restrictions on him and allowing him to hunt whenever the mood took him. While she didn't entirely approve of shooting things as a way of letting off steam, it definitely beat becoming the object of his terrifying rage and frustration. She didn't approve of wastefulness or killing big game at all, but he'd promised her that he never took down prey that was any bigger than she was, and after all, he made sure he always ate what he killed.

Chapter 69

Feeling slightly guilty for having leaned on super keen DC Badal for the majority of my recent legwork, I tackled the follow up on the car registrations from the Plymouth murders myself. The requests had been treated as a priority, and it quickly transpired that neither of the keepers from the time, or their immediate family, stacked up as likely suspects. A quick couple of calculations told me that former Sergeant Major Joseph Reilly-Dunstan would now be pushing a hundred years of age if he was alive, and that ex Conservative MP Michael Huntley-Sheridan would be almost ninety. Between them there was only one child, born to the Sergeant Major and his wife, and that was a daughter who would be in her early sixties now. I made a note to trace her details later for an informal chat on the off chance that she could offer something of value.

I weighed up my options and finally decided to check up on both the Major and the MP until I could formulate a better plan, knowing that if there was anything to find here then it certainly wasn't going to be a geriatric cannibal sneaking out of his nursing home at night to terrorise the city streets, but running out of viable options. On a whim I chose the army guy first, reasoning that there was a vague military link if I accepted the Naval theory that had come to dominate the hunt for a while at the time. An hour later I'd discovered that both the Sergeant Major and the MP had died some years previously, and that in the military guys case he was survived by a wife who was now very elderly, but according to the staff who tended to her at the

214

nursing home at least, was still entirely compos mentis. I thanked them for their time and help and scheduled an appointment to visit her the following day, feeling an indefinable sense of something which told me I was finally on the right track.

I fired off an email to Lee, who was out and about taking down details of a possible witness who swore that they'd seen Elizabeth Perry in a black Range Rover on the motorway hours after she'd gone missing, and got up to make coffee. I wanted him to help me look for links between any of the men from the Naval base who'd been routinely questioned all those years ago as the knot theory began to prevail, and the remaining names on my ragged looking and ever shrinking suspect list.

When I arrived back at my desk with the coffee I found myself with some time on my hands to kill, and decided to make a start myself while I waited for him to acknowledge me or return to the office, scanning my emails for one from Geeta which contained copies of those short voluntary interviews. I moved down the column of names first, hundreds of them all matching the vague description from a single eyewitness and all of them entirely unremarkable on the surface of things. I was looking for something that I recognised, perhaps a family surname that related to an offender that I knew, or that triggered an association with somebody involved in the Grey Man case, however peripherally. But nothing jumped off the screen at me.

I sighed and leaned back, taking a gulp from my over sized 'World's Best Aunt' cup, a present from Emily's children, sent through

215

the post rather than hand-delivered. It seemed like something of a joke at the time, on account of how little I got to see them, but I cherished it anyway and kept it at work where I spent the majority of my time. Finally I decided that I'd delayed for long enough, and I got down to the part that I'd been least looking forward to, starting alphabetically and opening up the first transcript from one of the Plymouth Naval interviews to begin the first of many long hours of reading.

Chapter 70

'It's always lovely to get visitors, not that it happens much these days my dear, but nevertheless it's wonderful that you're here.'

Mrs Jessie Reilly-Dunstan was a surprisingly sprightly but tiny lady of eighty six, who looked as if she'd dressed for an important occasion, with a cashmere wrap over a tailored looking cream top and beige slacks. She greeted me like an old friend, and I was enveloped in the scent of roses and vanilla from her perfume as she embraced me.

'It's a pleasure to meet you too Mrs Reilly-Dunstan. I'm Zara Wade, and I have to say already that I'm deeply envious of those pearls that you're wearing.'

I smiled and took the seat that she was guiding me onto, alongside her own and facing out over landscaped gardens and an open view of the countryside beyond the fence.

'Please call me Jessie, dear, it's been said before that Mrs Reilly-Dunstan is too big a name for such a small lady.'

She delivered a line that I imagined had been well-used over the decades, her eyes twinkling with pleasure at a private resonance that I wasn't privy too.

'Thank you Jessie, Zara's fine for me too, I only mention my rank when I'm being pretentious. I believe that you've already been made aware that I'm a Detective from Warwickshire, and that I'd like to ask you a few questions from back when you lived near Plymouth, if that's okay?'

I smiled and she nodded, looking out at the gardens rather than at me, but still giving me her attention.

'I remember the last one who came down to talk to me about then too. it would have been a few months ago now, I'm not precisely sure of the date since the days have a habit of falling into one another somewhat when you get to my age.'

She gave me a conspiratorial glance and then resumed her appraisal of the view.

'Another Detective came to see you? I don't suppose you can remember his name can you Jessie?'

I tried to mask my surprise, but did a bad job of it and the old lady picked it up immediately.

'That's one of the problems with modern day police forces, isn't it? The left hand doesn't know what the right hand's doing so they say.'

She patted my leg gently before continuing.

'Anyway, he wasn't a policeman. He was only helping the police, and he was a Doctor of some sort, a very pleasant chap who brought flowers with him. Not much of a looker, but if I was a few years younger I might have tried my luck anyway. Such good manners are very hard to come by these days, and I've learned to admire them much more than physical attributes in the course of my lifetime.'

She gave me a wink and I smiled again, trying to push away a sudden image of Alan Hardwick's ruined face when we'd found him.

'What did he want to know about exactly?'

I tried not hurry her along, but the words came out with an edge of urgency that made her look up at me and pause before she spoke again.

'He wanted to know about Joseph's car of all things, a great big old Jaguar it was, and his pride and joy, he used to polish it to such a sheen as you wouldn't believe. You could barely look at it on a sunny day.'

I felt the growing sense of anticipation again, I was firmly back on the right track.

'It sounds like he was a very fastidious man. Was there anything else he wanted to know about it, Jessie?'

I kept my eyes trained on her expression, watching her delve into her memory banks for details of the conversation.

'Yes, he asked about Madeleine too. That's our daughter, or perhaps I should say that was our daughter until she chose to disown us. I haven't seen her in a very long time now.'

I struggled for another question, striving to see the significance of the daughter in all this, but then Jessie volunteered more information and pulled the veil away for me.

'She chose him over the life that we could have provided her with. A Navy boy with a less than distinguished service record and a foul temper to go with it too. Not that you'd have suspected it to begin with when you first met him, he was always so charming to our faces. Joseph even let him borrow the car from time to time, which was nothing short of a miracle. But he was a bad seed through and through, Zara, my daughter's face told us that when we got wise to the fact that he was hitting her and tried to separate them. Then when he got his inheritance he packed it all in and took her away from us to travel here there and everywhere with the money burning a hole in his pocket, and there was nothing that we could do about it.'

Chapter 71

When I left the grounds of Jessie's expensive nursing home my mind was spinning with what she had shared with me. I now knew that Doctor Alan Hardwick had been here before me and heard what the old lady had to say about the man that was in all likelihood responsible for a chain of serial killings that spanned more than three decades. My heart sank at how a man with a proud record of helping us to catch these monsters could keep a revelation like this to himself, and allow the Grey Man to carry on murdering and mutilating as frequently as he desired. I knew that Hardwick's financial difficulties had forced him towards acts of increasing desperation, but in my mind he was now complicit in the two murders besides his own that had occurred since he'd managed to solve this puzzle. The darkest reaches of my thoughts couldn't help feeling that he'd gotten his just desserts.

Oddly Jessie hadn't been able to recall the full name of the man who had stolen her daughter away, just that his first name was John and that he'd been in the Navy up until the time that he received a very large inheritance from his parent's estate. But perhaps I was being uncharitable since there'd been a lot of years pass since then. If her reckoning on the dates was accurate then he'd received the money shortly after the fifth and final Plymouth murder, and then left to visit a string of far flung destinations. She didn't know how long he'd been abroad with Madeleine for exactly, because of the breakdown in communications with her daughter that had followed them leaving. But they'd have had the means and the time to be able to holiday at will over the years that followed. My skin crawled at what 'John' might have been able to get away with in a string of countries as he'd travelled and lived in the lap of luxury. There were many parts of the world where affluence bought immunity from suspicion and police officials could be paid to look the other way if they ever came knocking, and I felt a quiet fury as I promised justice for the unknown dead.

I climbed back into the car and left the radio silent as I pulled away, thinking now about Lee's question from in the office as we'd bounced ideas around the other day. What defines our murders would you say? That they're very controlled and planned as a general rule, obsessively so, and that they revolve around food and dining.

The food and dining was the clue that I'd missed the significance of. It was much more specific than that, his choice of methods was showing us whereabouts he'd been in the world. The sushi rolls, roasting over spits and open air char grilling of parts of his victims were like a sick in joke, advertising places he'd been and their respective cuisines, and with the possible exception of the dead Doctor, we'd all missed its significance completely.

I wondered whether he was disappointed by our ineptitude, and whether acts such as the staging of scenes and the 'gift' of Elizabeth Perry's head being made up to look like my own were his way of trying to prompt us further along the right path? I'd read before about how some of these types of murderer subconsciously wanted to be caught and prevented from committing more crimes, and my mind turned again to the creepy letters that he was leaving for me, in which he drew comparisons between us. If he did want to be caught then it was specifically me that he wanted to be the one to come knocking on his door, that much was becoming clear. I turned right out of the end of the long driveway and accelerated along the road that took me back towards the motorway, knowing that when I arrived back I would be armed with the information to finally uncover his identity and finish this thing. The only question besides that remaining now was what exactly what the nature of that connection to me was?

Chapter 72

The Grey Man listened to the sounds of Madeleine and the girls going about their daily routines in the house without him from his vantage point up in the loft, and felt a sense of nervous excitement descending over everything again. He had been up here for almost twenty four hours, but the space was exceedingly well insulated and had a small discreet fridge with modest provisions inside, so he was relatively comfortable after his eyes adjusted to the absence of light. He'd planned for this day for some time, even though he had often kidded himself that it might never come, but now the end of everything was finally in sight he felt at peace with the monster inside.

The discussions with his wife of so many years the previous evening had been the final deciding factor for him, along with the growing realisation that his control over the part of himself that lived to maim and kill was disappearing from view. He couldn't go on, and now was the time to make that decision on his own terms.

He waited until late afternoon, existing in a state of near meditative contemplation, and watching mental re-runs of his career highlights on repeat on the vast imaginary screen that his eyes projected for him. Finally the quality of the meagre light that crept in through small slits in between the roof tiles began to change perceptibly, and the movements down below took on a more sluggish note that suggested bed time for Lexie and Annabel was approaching. He waited for the sound of running water to come as

Madeleine filled the large free standing bath tub with its clawed lion's feet, followed by the rapid patter of bare feet across the wooden floor, and then he began to stir, rubbing feeling back into temporarily immobile limbs to get the circulation flowing again.

He lifted up the hatch and lowered the loft ladder down noiselessly through the hole, until it rested on the rug that neatly filled the floor space beneath and prevented any contact between the foot of the ladder and the polished floors that would have advertised his presence. The girls were splashing around now, giggling uncontrollably over something and nothing like normal children were apt to do. Of course his own upbringing had been devoid of laughter, so the sound was all but meaningless to him. He stepped over one of the boards that usually squeaked under foot and pushed the door open with his foot, as he rearranged a loop of knotted rope into the required shape with a deftness born of considerable practice.

He had been expecting to see the back of his wife bent down low over the tub applying shampoo or conditioner to the girls hair, but for some reason she was sitting over on the closed toilet lid, which put her a good six feet away from where he'd been planning to ambush her. The extra seconds delay as he realised that fact gave her the opportunity to see the rope in his hands first and react, and to his intense surprise and her credit she did just that, snatching up a ceramic dish and hurling it straight at the centre of his forehead with considerable force, propelling him back out of the doorway. He forced himself forwards again, dazed and with blood running down into his eyes, and jammed his bare foot into the gap between door and frame a moment before she threw herself against it to try to keep him out.

The pain was intense and he made a noise like a wounded bull but kept his foot wedged in place and slowly pushed his way in. Both girls were screaming fit to burst, striving to press themselves as far back into the corner of the bath as possible and wrapping the shower curtain around themselves, and Madeleine lashed out at him again, trying to get her nails into his eyes, fighting for their sakes if not her own. He batted her arm away and punched her hard in the face, feeling something crunch and tasting his own flowing blood on his lips as she fell.

'I was going to spare you some of what they will face for old time's sake, but I believe that moment's passed us by now dear.'

He said in a low hiss, looping the rope around her neck and starting to pull it tight.

Chapter 73

By the time that I'd arrived back in Warwickshire the sun was dropping down below the horizon and painting the landscape in shades of red and gold. It should have been the end of my shift for the day, but I was still in the hold of my intense excitement at discovering what Hardwick had been holding back from us before he was killed. I'd managed to raise Lee on his mobile phone as I drove back, for once using the fiddly to fit hands free kit that was standard issue in unmarked police vehicles these days, and he was picking out a list of 'John's' from the hundreds of short interview transcripts that we'd begun wading through the previous day. I secretly prayed that by some miracle there'd only be one man named John on the list.

Gripped by new urgency, I virtually ran up the stairs to the top floor of the police building, which was probably an infinitely more dangerous pursuit than tracking down murderers and rapists, considering the threadbare state of some of the carpet and the fact that I was wearing heels. As I entered the offices I noted that Geeta Badal had elected to stay behind too, her keen instincts evidently alerting her to the prospect of something interesting to get her teeth into, although she was not yet in the loop about what was keeping Lee and myself here late.

'What have you got so far, Lee?' I asked breathlessly, seeing stray curls of my hair performing interesting feats in my peripheral vision, and catching Geeta openly listening to what was being said.

'There were eleven John's to begin with, but I've already been able to narrow it down to six due to a couple of premature deaths and another couple staying at Her Majesty's Pleasure at the time of some of the offences. Do you recognise any of the names?'

I leaned over and scanned down them quickly, feeling a surge of disappointment and confusion that none of them seemed remotely familiar to me. So what was the connection to me? Perhaps we'd managed to convince ourselves that we'd seen something that wasn't really there to see.

'Geeta?'

I watched her flinch fractionally at the unexpected use of her name, before she swiftly regained control of herself.

'Ma'am?'

She sat bolt upright, looking poised for action, her eyes locked onto me in readiness.

'Are you able to obtain details of marriages registered on your system, based solely on a maiden name?'

I'd usually made enquiries directly with various registrars and records offices, as I'd been taught to do, but I remembered that many of these records had now been computerised, and techno savvy newer officers gathered much of their information in an investigation without leaving their desks.

'Yes, Ma'am. What name am I looking for?'

She looked down at her keyboard and began to access the necessary parts of the system in preparation.

'Madeleine Reilly-Dunstan.'

I spelled out the names, mindful of the various different possibilities and paused to allow her to complete the screens, holding my breath in anticipation.

'Okay, let's see what we get back.'

She tapped more keys and read briefly before tapping away some more. The sound of the printer at the end of the desk started up as she looked up.

'I've printed out the most likely looking entry. It looks like they got married in Plymouth quite a lot of years ago. Does this relate to the Grey Man case, Ma'am?'

I debated my options for a split second and decided that her hard work deserved to be rewarded.

'Yes it does. Any chance of you doing an electoral register search for a last known address on her too?' I said snatching the single sheet off the printer and scanning the details of the entry. I stopped when I reached the end and immediately went back over it, reading again to make sure that my eyes weren't playing tricks on me. The sound of rushing blood suddenly filling my ears with white noise.

'Zara, are you alright?'

Lee must have seen something terrible in my face, because he forgot to address me formally and reached out to take the sheet from my hands, scanning the details for himself.

'I don't understand...' he began.

'They did something unusual with their surnames, Lee. They combined the Reilly part of hers with Moore from his to make Reimoore, which was enough for me to miss him in the list.'

229

I stopped and looked at first him and then Geeta, who had stopped typing.

'John Reimoore is my sister's father-in-law, I've met him on several occasions. That's what the connection between him and me is.'

Chapter 74

The Grey Man placed his securely bound wife in the boot of the Jaguar and closed the lid down hard, before returning to the rear passenger's seats of the car and ensuring that the woollen blanket covering the girls was still in place. It was highly unlikely that they would be stopped on their short drive up to the cottage, so doubtless these modest precautions were entirely unnecessary, but he didn't want to risk disaster at this late stage of proceedings. As a backup he had a loaded crossbow and a large bowie knife within easy reach in the front of the car, and he was an expert with both. Anybody stopping him this evening wouldn't live for long enough to realise their mistake.

He got in and started the engine, ignoring the sounds from the youngest girl under the blanket, who had not been able to control her hysteria for long enough to avoid the need for tape across the mouth. The eldest had been far more amenable, accepting her situation much more readily with only the occasional fit of sobbing. Why did they so often cry, scream and plead when it was patently obvious that those actions carried absolutely no meaning for him at all?

He remembered one of the earliest targets, a spoilt little faux rich girl away from home and her parent's money, ridiculously easily flattered and seduced by the prospect of a sugar daddy with a bottomless wallet. Please don't kill me, I'll do anything that you want me to, I don't want to die. She'd said when she'd seen the selection of shining steel cleavers. Her arms had been tied tightly to her sides and he could still recall the mascara tears that were running all the way down both cheeks. She'd parted her legs slightly under his gaze, as if that had been what he was after, and as if he couldn't have taken it with her consent simply by taking her back to a room in a plush sweet and plying her with champagne for the evening. You'll do anything that I want you to anyway. He'd replied and begun to slice ignoring the piercing shrieks.

A thumping noise from the boot told him that Madeleine was starting to regain her senses, but nobody would be there to hear it over the rumble over the engine on darkened country roads. She'd surprised and pleased him with the ferocity of her attack back in the house, and he'd had to close the deep wound on his forehead with surgical tape from the first aid box before once he'd got the three of them safely secured.

He listened to the gravel crunching satisfyingly underneath the wheels as they moved along the grand driveway and up to the electric gates with their clever sensors. He'd had this home built to his own specifications when the wanderlust had subsided and he'd decided that it was time to put down roots and get back into the world of business again. Madeleine had not been involved in the choosing of the site, he'd only permitted her to begin visiting when the old building had been removed and the new one was nearing completion. So she'd die never knowing that the land had once housed an abattoir, and that the ground she walked over each day was saturated with decade's worth of blood and suffering.

As a boy he'd been taken to such places on countless occasions when his father had decided that one of their 'trips' was in order. Mother had always remained at home, never arguing with John Moore senior, and the old man had taken a keen interest in spending time with him, moulding the boy in his own twisted and violent image. Can you smell that, John? His father would ask, breathing in deep lungs full of the slaughterhouse air, and he'd followed suit, nostrils heavy with the smell of death. That's the smell of cattle becoming meat, John, and it's what we're made from too. There are many places around the world where people used to eat each other as food, and in famines and wars it sometimes still happens. What do you suppose we taste like?

Ten years later they'd hunted a girl with crossbows and knives together in remote woodland, and he'd let the boy find out the answer to that question for himself.

Chapter 75

John Reimoore, a man who I'd looked in the face and berated for the behaviour of his only son, was an horrific murderer of the worst kind, a psychopath and a cannibal who'd been killing for decades and never been caught. He was also the joint temporary custodian of my sister's two young girls, Lexie and Annabel. My first instinct had been to rush straight out to arrest him, but Lee and Geeta had insisted on organising an armed response unit to take care of the entry to his home and the subsequent apprehension of one of the most dangerous men imaginable. Now all that could be done was to wait and hope, passing the time by looking back into any surviving records that detailed the life of a monster who had hidden in our midst.

I read back over what Geeta had been able to find for me with her superior computer skills, while she went to make coffee and Lee headed for the toilets. In a relatively short period of time we'd been able to establish that he'd been dishonourably discharged from the Navy a short while before his widowed father, John Moore Senior, had passed away suddenly and left him the heir to a sprawling country manor and a significant fortune. With the benefit of hindsight the timing of his father's death at the precise point that John junior had most needed money was convenient to say the least, and I made a note to look very closely into the pathologists report at a later stage. Unfortunately, I had no authority to access records about military service and the circumstances of his discharge from duty, but

I'd bet my house on it being related to violence against a woman or more than one.

Tired of waiting for news from the guys with guns, I delved further into Reimoore's affairs, striving to build up a picture of where he'd been and what assets he'd managed to acquire over the years with the benefit of all that money. He'd bought his way into the computing company that he now sat on as an Executive Director of some variety, and I realised sadly that it was the same company that Elizabeth Perry had innocently chosen to work for, not knowing that a predator with a taste for flesh sat watching her from his office and planning her death. Detectives from my office had been interviewing friends and colleagues, since I'd been engaged in following up other leads, so Reimoore's name hadn't yet struck a chord with anybody. He'd also built the home that he lived in with Madeleine using the proceeds from the sale of his old family residence, as well as purchasing property overseas in Morocco and France, and a cottage, that was extremely modest for his tastes judging by the sale price compared to the others, that was only a stone's throw away in the Warwickshire countryside.

Geeta arrived back with coffee and I thanked her for it, advising her that she could go home to rest if she wished, since it seemed that none of us would be directly involved in the Grey Man's capture now, but that her efforts had not gone unnoticed.

I knew that Geeta's home was only five minutes by car from here, and that she'd engineered it to be that way once she'd been accepted for CID, selling up the place that she'd shared with a fiancé

235

who was now no longer on the scene, and essentially marrying herself to the job instead. They don't tell you what it will cost you, do they? I remembered the line from one of the Grey Man letters and had to bite down on the urge to lecture DC Badal on the importance of having something else to live for outside of work as she walked out of the door without a backwards glance.

I sipped my coffee and let my eyes wander back over the screen again as Lee re-entered the office drying his hands on his trousers.

'I don't suppose you're still awake enough to run one more errand with me tonight before we go home?'

I asked, looking sheepish.

'Go on then. But you'll have to make it up to me later. Where are we going?'

He smiled lasciviously to emphasise his intent for the payback.

'Reimoore has a country cottage not far from here, which strikes me as slightly odd for a man who already lives out in the sticks and has the money to go anywhere he chooses. I'd like a nose around there before we call it a day.'

Chapter 76

It was pitch black in the boot of the car, darker than she had thought possible, with the choking smell of petrol all around and the tape over her mouth half suffocating her. Grandma Madeleine truly believed she was as close to hell as she'd ever been. The car bounced up and down over the bumpy road surface, travelling at speed and pitching her against the hard sides of the confined space, bruising every square inch of her body. She guessed from the movements that they were out in the countryside somewhere on unpaved roads, and her mind immediately focussed on the little cottage that they owned but seldom used. Her next though was about the crossbow and assortment of knives for skinning, gutting and filleting that were kept there.

All kinds of associations that had sat dormant in her memory, stubbornly ignored because of what acknowledging them would have meant, began to resurface as she rode the waves of pain and fought to pull enough oxygen into her lungs through the one nostril that remained unblocked to survive.

She thought first of the dead girl in their bathroom back in Plymouth, a mere scrap of a thing covered in bruises with her sightless eyes bulging. He'd stood before her then looking tearful and vulnerable, his whole world unravelling before his eyes and looking towards her for something that would make it alright again. I didn't mean to, he'd said, and she'd acted on autopilot, finding something much colder inside herself than she'd wanted to acknowledge quickly emerging and taking charge. She could not allow this girl to ruin what they were building, not when they had so much to lose. She'd found herself fiercely scrubbing the tub and tiles with every type of scouring cloth and chemical that she could find, while her fiancé had been out in their car finding somewhere remote to dump the dead body of a strange girl wrapped in polythene.

The uncomfortable silence between them that had followed stretched out into days and weeks. With him immersing himself in work, and her keeping herself busy around the house and taking comfort in the feeling of the baby that was inside her growing and growing each day. She didn't want to think about it now, but gradually the images from that night had begun to fade away. She could try to attribute it to the fog of late pregnancy descending if she liked, but deep down she knew that just wasn't the case. The truth was that she had simply pushed those events to one side as an inconvenience, consigning them to a history that would not be revisited and separating them neatly from the things that mattered in her little world.

Tears pricked at the corners of her eyes and she panicked for a moment as she found herself temporarily unable to breathe again, blowing hard out of her nostrils to clear them and then inhaling as hard as she could, feeling dizzy and nauseous. She'd ignored the actions of a monster, and she'd ignored other patterns of behaviour over the years that told her he'd not stopped at just the one. She'd been set on convincing herself that there was always a reasonable explanation for the mist of blood on his clothing as it went into the wash, or the smell of smoke and petrol in his hair.

The car hit another rut in the dirt road, and she was tossed back against the rear of one of the headlight casings, feeling something hard and sharp tear a shallow wound in her scalp, and clenching her teeth against the flare of pain. It was a few more seconds of guilt and self pitying thoughts before she realised what that meant. A sharp edge could cut through the ropes that bound her hands together. A sharp edge meant the possibility of freedom. Grandma Madeleine might have been complicit in the deaths of numerous young women by virtue of her wilful inability to see what kind of creature her husband was. But she promised herself now that she would save the lives of the two terrified girls inside the car, even if it was at the cost of her own.

Chapter 77

'Sorry to be a pain, Za, but do you think we can stop and grab something to eat before we continue our quest up into the back end of beyond? I'm absolutely starving.'

Lee was thinking about his stomach as usual, and as I pushed aside my irritation I had to remind myself that it had been hours since any of us had last eaten, so I could hardly blame him for that. We were back in the Volvo and cutting a sweeping path across the dark B-roads that circled the inner city areas, so it wouldn't be too far out of our way to pull in for a quick bite anyway.

'No problem. where are you thinking of?'

I kept my eyes trained on the road ahead in case my expression involuntarily advertised the fact that, despite what I was saying, it was in fact a problem for me, but thankfully he didn't seem to notice.

'There's a good Chinese place round this side somewhere I think. take the next right and go left at the bottom and I'll guide you in from there.' He said, pointing the direction seemingly just in case I'd forgotten which way right was.

'Yes sir. I presume the tip will be good when we arrive at our destination though, sir?' I replied sarcastically. If he was going to speak to me like I was a cabbie then I was sure as hell going to pull him up on it.

'If there's a problem with that then I don't mind waiting.'

He looked at me quizzically, and I caught his expression as I glanced in the rear view mirror.

'No…sorry. I'm just pissed that I'm not up there breaking down the door and slapping on the leg irons is all. We've both worked so hard on this case for so long that it seems somehow unfair that we're being robbed of closure, especially since he's been writing to me all the way through.'

I blew a stream of air up my forehead in an attempt to move the long curl that dangled in my eye line, and flicked on the indicator preparing to take a side road back in towards civilisation.

'You know what? You're right. Let's run this errand first and eat afterwards. We might both feel better when we know that we've done everything that we can.'

He reached out and turned the indicator back off, grinning knowingly as I made a move to swipe his hand away.

'It's a deal mister. I'll even spring for something fancier than a takeaway if it's not past your bedtime already? There's a late night Southern Indian place across town that I've been meaning to try for a while now.'

I looked across and we shared a small smile, the brief moment of tension between us evaporating as quickly as it had appeared.

Free to concentrate on the task at hand again I moved back over into the outside lane, and took a turning out towards open fields and dry stone walls, although the darkness obscured the fine detail of everything that fell beyond the reach of the headlight beams. The roads nearest to habitation were streaked with smears of road kill, much of it looking as if it had been hit only recently. Evidently it was a bad night to be out on the roads.

'So what are you hoping that we're going to find when we get to this cottage of his?'

Lee's voice unexpectedly broke the stream of my thoughts and I paused to consider the question.

'It could be anything; knives, rope, trophies that he kept back for himself from the victims. There might even be whatever he used to mince up Elizabeth's body out here. Basically all of the things that he's unlikely to be keeping around the house.'

We were all officially working on the assumption that he'd been acting alone on these horrific crimes, but we both knew that, although a rarity, there was a possibility that his wife was involved in some way. If that assumption was right then there could be a whole Aladdin's cave of horrors waiting for us, in which case we'd call it in and preserve the scene for CSI rather than risk trampling all over items that might be needed to secure a successful conviction. My thoughts wandered again to Lexie and Annabel living blissfully unaware in the care of a monster. Hopefully by now they'd be on their way into the safety of police custody as the monster was taken down in chains.

Chapter 78

In the dark stifling space Grandma Madeleine manoeuvred the rope binding her hands together over the sharp spike of hard plastic again, snagging the cord and working through another few precious threads before she was pitched off line and felt the point gouging into her wrists and forearms again. She could feel the blood flowing freely down the insides of her arms, and the carpet in the boot was warm and wet where her face rested in it, but faced with no other choice she continued to persevere, knowing that at any moment they could arrive at their destination and her efforts would have all been in vain.

She positioned the weakening ties back over the cutting edge again and chewed at the tape over her mouth; it was wet from saliva, snot and blood, and the combination was causing it to pull away at one corner, making it easier to draw in more precious oxygen to her lungs. As if on cue the last of the adhesive gave way and she was able to spit it onto the floor, savouring one deep breath before she realised what that meant. Now her teeth were free to work on the fraying rope too. Maybe just maybe she could get out of here alive, but failing that she'd go for his eyes with her nails and his throat with her teeth - leave him incapacitated for long enough to grab the keys and drive the girls away from harm.

Thoughts of escape spurred her on, and she alternated between using the plastic spike to rip through parts of the cord and tearing at it with her teeth like a crazed animal. She'd been fastidious about her appearance her whole life. It had been one of the things that had attracted him to her in the first place, when he'd sauntered over to her side full of confidence and charm, picking her to spend his nights with out of all of the girls in the dark club where the Navy boys came when they were on leave. Now though she couldn't have cared less about how she looked though, as she felt a tooth coming loose from the effort of chewing tough fibres apart and carried on regardless. Now it was about survival pure and simple, everything else was completely unimportant.

After what felt like an eternity, the last strands finally gave way, and she was able to use both hands freely again. She adjusted herself into a different position and rubbed some feeling back into her wrists, feeling the blood returning now that there was nothing cutting into them anymore. She tried to ignore the weeping gashes and the pain that struck like lightning every time she clenched her fists, and set to work on untying the tight knots that fastened her ankles together, knowing that she'd need as much mobility as possible when the boot lid was opened. There's only going to be one shot at this, get it wrong and all three of us are going to die horribly. Don't you dare hesitate and kid yourself that he cares for you for even a second, or that small chance will be gone.

The car began to slow down perceptibly, bouncing heavily from side to side on its axles, and forcing her to push her arms and legs against the sides of the space to avoid more bruising impacts with the hard surfaces that were all around. Deprived of the ability to see anything by the ink thick darkness Madeleine was able to conjure up a clear mental picture of the trail that led up to the cottage, even thought she had not visited for sometime. She vividly recalled the deep ruts in the dirt track where the road disappeared from view and the small stone building came into view. They were here already.

She thought about where his face would be when he opened up to fetch her out and planned her spring, but no matter how hard she tried to force it, she couldn't make her mind show her winning the physical confrontation. He was not a big man by most people's standards, but he was bigger than her and deceptively strong, and therefore much more than a match for anything she might throw at him. The only thing she had on her side was a fraction of a second's head start before he realised that she'd managed to get her hands and feet free, but she was weak from blood loss and sick to the stomach with motion sickness, hardly at her fighting best. She scoured her brain for some other kind of advantage she could manufacture, thinking about the sharp bit of plastic and wondering whether it could be pulled loose, before it finally hit her. There was a heavy metal jack in a compartment underneath the carpet in the back corner of the boot.

Chapter 79

The roads got progressively worse as we drove further away from the comforting glow of the maze of city streets and out into rural emptiness. I was forced to slow the car to a crawl in places to avoid scraping the underside on yet another hidden hollow. I was already half convinced that I'd caused some kind of catastrophic damage to it anyway, due to the metallic clang that had accompanied my overenthusiastic rallying back where the tarmac had given way to a patchwork of cracks and potholes. I'd not given consideration to how hard it was going to be to navigate our way up to a remote cottage on narrow unlit and unfamiliar country lanes in the dark either, and I was starting to lose the firm belief that I was on the right track.

'So I'm guessing that you've committed the turns we've been taking to memory somehow?'

Lee was wearing a look of pure mischief, so I knew that he'd recognised my growing uncertainty, but I wasn't about to admit that my knowledge of the area extended to a glance at an internet map and little else.

'We're going the right way; it's set back slightly from the road in woodland judging by the maps that I viewed, and it'll be completely in darkness, so we're not going to see it until we're right on top of it.'

I injected a note of confidence that I didn't truly feel into my voice and nodded enthusiastically as if to emphasise the point.

'Actually I was thinking more about how we find our way back down again afterwards. I don't really fancy having to choose between spending the night in the car, or in a killer's holiday home, when we realise we can't retrace our steps.'

He was grinning as he said it, but he had a point, and I scrabbled for a comeback.

'We're higher up here, in case that's escaped your attention? Which means that we'll be able to see where the streetlights begin again. If we're not a hundred percent on the turnings to take then we simply head for the light.'

I made a motion with my hand as if I was wafting him away from me, and grinned in triumph, taking my eyes off the road for a moment.

'Okay, okay, I'll give you that one. Say, watch out for that...'

He didn't get to finish the sentence, and I hit the brakes as we were both violently jolted around in our seats and a loud bang followed by disconcerting rattling came from underneath the car.

I'd been concentrating too hard on getting one up on Lee, and not enough on the fact that my speed had begun to creep steadily back up again. As I'd looked at him to deliver my killer line, I'd failed to notice a monster of a rut in the road where the last broken up fragments of tarmac finally gave way to hard earth. The result was that the bottom of the car had smacked down hard against the solid ground, and judging by the sounds that were now coming from it, the damage was probably terminal.

'Shit.'

I said and brought the car to a standstill, switching off the engine and getting out to have a look, closely followed by Lee. Not that either of us knew enough about the mechanical workings of cars to do anything for it if the news was as bad as I was expecting, but still I wanted to see what we were dealing with.

'Ouch! That doesn't look too promising, does it?'

Lee gave a low whistle and pointed at a section of something hanging down at the front of the car, visible in the radius of the headlight beams.

'No, it doesn't. you know what you were saying about spending the night up here?'

I tried to make light of the situation, after all, police vehicles got damaged on frequent occasions and we both had our phones to arrange a lift back to civilisation if we needed one.

'Za?'

Something in Lee's voice made me look up sharply, and I followed the line of his gaze along the track in front of our damaged car.

'Oh,' was all I could manage as I spotted it too.

Parked at the dark roadside a mere fifty yards away was the rear of another car, a silver Jaguar with its boot lid open. Beyond the Jaguar, surrounded by trees that hung their branches down over the roof, was a small stone cottage. A weak but conspicuous light was visible in one of the windows.

Chapter 80

'Okay. What do we do now?'

Lee looked at me helplessly, knowing that this new development could mean one of many things.

'Call it in and request urgent back up. We'll worry about making fools of ourselves later.' I replied.

My mind raced with possibilities. Was the presence of the silver Jaguar innocent, somebody staying out here in a holiday let, completely unaware that the landlord was a vicious murdering psychopath, or was this the Grey Man himself, and if so did he have the girls up here too?

I searched my memory banks for the make and model of his car but came up blank. I'd had no reason to remember those details, as far as I'd been concerned he was on his way into police custody at the end of several gun barrels now. I dithered and hesitated, changing my mind repeatedly while Lee calmly communicated our position and discovery to control. His voice carried for some distance in the absence of other background noise, and I was hyper aware that anybody in the cottage would probably have heard the car approaching and now the sound of our voices. We'd well and truly lost any element of surprise, but we hadn't thought that we'd need it.

'If it's him and they're in there…' I began, feeling sick and panicky.

'Look, we don't know that, and even if he was up here that's not to say that he's got the girls with him. From what we've come to understand about him they're not his type either.'

He pulled a face at the clumsiness of the words and apologised with his eyes.

'Why the fuck haven't we been updated on what's going on at the main residence? This is my damned investigation, and now I'm sat here utterly in the dark and facing an impossible situation.'

I couldn't stop the bitterness in my tone, even though I knew I was being completely unfair. The armed officers hadn't known what we were planning, and the decision to come up here had been my call. If we were in a dangerous predicament the blame for that rested squarely and exclusively on my own shoulders.

'I won't ask you to come in with me, Lee, but I can't just stand here and face the possibility that a maniac is inside butchering my nieces.'

I turned and began to walk towards the cottage, not daring to check if he was following, but absurdly grateful when I felt him drop into step on my right shoulder.

'It's not going to be him. We're going to burst in on a young couple out here for some private quality time.'

He didn't look at me as he spoke, and I heard the tremor of apprehension where his voice strained at the end of the sentence. I knew he was attempting to convince himself as much as me, and that no matter how much we both wanted it to be true it seemed farfetched. Unlike our counterparts overseas and our colleagues on armed response, we did not have guns to unholster and tasers to render an attacker senseless in seconds. We'd be walking in without even a set of handcuffs between us, having left them locked up at the HQ at the official end of our shift, and that could be a costly mistake.

We walked the remaining distance to the silver car in silence, trying to keep our footsteps as quiet as possible by walking on the sparse grass lining the sides of the dirt trail, even though it seemed unlikely that our presence had gone unnoticed. Lee produced a key fob with a small intense torch beam built into it when we were ten yards away, and shone it directly into the open boot.

'Oh God, please no.' I whispered softly to myself, like it might make what I was seeing magically disappear.

The body carpet inside the boot had once been a shade of light grey I guessed, but it was now almost entirely covered in a dark liquid that stained the fabric black. As if any doubt remained about what that liquid was, streaks of bright red ran down the back of the car itself and small pools had formed and then clotted in various places on the ground below. What we were looking at was a significant amount of somebody's blood.

Chapter 81

Madeleine was in the bathtub to keep the mess to a minimum, she was not yet dead, but the usual rhythmic rise and fall of her chest had been replaced by a weaker fluttering motion that experience told him meant it was just a matter of time now. Even if she did wake up fleetingly she was not going to be in any kind of state to attempt a repetition of what she had managed when he'd opened up the car boot earlier. There'd been a fleeting moment as his eyes transmitted the information to his brain in which he'd failed to realise that she'd somehow managed to get free of the ties that bound her hands and feet, and that she was swinging the heavy metal car jack towards his head with blurring speed. Only the instinctive flinch away at the recognition of unexpected motion had saved him from having his head smashed open, but she'd still managed to connect solidly with his collarbone, and now one arm hung limp and useless at his side and a tidal wave of pain swept through him every few seconds when he moved.

He'd been unarmed when she'd attacked him, but the force of the swing with the weight of the metal object had pitched her head first out of the car and onto the hard floor. In momentarily indescribable agony he'd only been able to muster sufficient force to stamp once on her wrist to force her to release the weapon, feeling the delicate bones cracking underneath his foot, and then twice more on her bloodied face as she'd rolled over to look up at him, all of her strength utterly spent.

Once the girls were safely stowed in the locked metal shed at the rear of the property, he'd been able to return to her in order to drag her indoors and clumsily into the bathroom. He wasn't concerned about the possibility of her battered body drawing attention, since it was vanishingly unlikely that they'd be disturbed out here, particularly at this hour; but he hadn't wanted to risk her coming back to a state of sufficient consciousness to mount another attack when he least expected it. After all, there was still work to be done. He'd expended a huge amount of energy in getting her limp from inside the cottage, and even more when he'd stopped part way and lost control of himself, kicking and stamping her in a frenzy until the feelings of rage had passed, and it was that which had put her in her present rapidly deteriorating condition.

'Don't die on me yet, dear. Not before I finish preparing the girls anyway.' He said, watching her closely, half anticipating that her eyes would suddenly flick back open despite her injuries suggesting otherwise.

He left her then, gritting his teeth against another sweeping wave of pain and cursing the stupid woman, taking time to lean against the doorframe before finally getting a handle on it and heading back out to the locked metal shed in the garden. As he got closer he could hear one of them sobbing again, while the other one whispered gently to her, the sobbing getting louder as he fumbled with the lock one handed and opened the door.

'Almost time to eat girls, so let's have you out of there now.'

He watched as neither of them moved, huddling together in the corner and staring at him with wide eyes.

'What have you done with Grandma?' Asked Lexie in a loud obstinate tone.

'She's in the bath at the moment, but she'll be joining us later. Now get up and come outside.'

This time he didn't disguise the menace in the instruction, leaving them under no illusions that they would be risking his wrath if they didn't comply. The youngest girl ignored him and looked at her sister for guidance, who slowly nodded as she climbed to her feet.

The drone of an engine reached his ears and he held up a hand for them to stay where they were, cocking his head to one side to be sure. Definitely the sound of a car approaching. As he continued to listen he heard a loud bang, the vehicle bottoming out on a rut in the road, followed by the noise of the engine dying. He quickly shoved the girls back inside, pushing the door back to with his shoulder while he manipulated the lock back into place. It was probably nothing, but it was late and he'd never been disturbed out here before, which limited the likely options for who it could be.

Chapter 82

The front door was slightly ajar, with textbook bloody drag marks running all the way from the rear of the car into the hallway, which lay in darkness. The only illumination was provided by the beam of blue-white light from Lee's miniature torch. Somebody had moved the body of another person who was either dead or dying through this way, and since I was pretty sure that the property was owned by one of the worst serial killers in living memory, I was willing to take a wild stab at John Reimoore being somewhere inside waiting for us.

'I'm going in first; no arguments.'

Lee placed his arm across the front of me as he spoke, but if he'd thought that I was going to protest then he was wrong. Old-fashioned chivalry was more than welcome right now.

'Okay, but if he starts stabbing make sure you hang on and keep him occupied for long enough for me to make good my escape, right?'

It felt wrong joking at a time like this, but it had the desired effect of alleviating some of the fear that held me in a tight cold grip, and I caught the quick flash of white as Lee smiled in appreciation and recognition.

'When he makes his move we both rush him and take him down. Armed or not he'll be hard pressed to deal with an attack from the two of us simultaneously.'

Lee's expression settled back into seriousness. He practiced Taekwondo and Boxing in his spare time, and I'd done some Judo back in my early twenties, but neither of us was exactly a martial arts expert. In fact, based on my dismal performance when David had pushed his way into my home, I could do with some more lessons. I made a mental note that I'd get some if I walked away from this more or less intact.

'Fine.'

I put in a silent prayer that armed response would arrive as back up some time right around now. The irony of the fact that I'd envied them the task of apprehending the Grey Man up until a few minutes ago was not entirely lost on me, but I'd relocate the finer points of my sense of humour later on when I wasn't shaking with adrenaline.

'Oh, and look for something to arm yourself with as soon as we're inside, we'll worry about reasonable and proportionate force after we finish beating him senseless.'

He tipped me a wink to say that the last part was offered at least partly in jest, but it was a good idea nevertheless, and then he nudged the door further open and swept the torchlight around inside, scanning every available corner before we entered.

I stayed up close to his back, trying to convince myself that I was not utterly terrified by this situation, trying to remind myself that I was the lead detective in a major murder enquiry and as such I wasn't allowed to let fear cloud my judgement or get in the way of making the arrest, and forcing myself to stand fully upright. Why did I feel like a frightened little girl again then? Because usually you're bringing them in on your own terms, fully prepared and with back up to spare. Not stumbling across them through pure dumb luck with the strong possibility that the lives of your own loved ones are at stake if you mess it all up.

I grabbed Lee's shoulder as he took the first step through the doorway, halting him in his tracks. He stopped and looked back at me quizzically, scanning the area over my shoulder as if he expected our killer to leap out into view brandishing a bloody knife and a human head.

'What is it?'

He dropped his eyes back down to meet my own.

'There's a chance that my nieces are here, and judging by all of the blood it doesn't look good. I want you to promise me that if something goes wrong and we're too late, or I get hurt here before I can take him down, then you'll make him pay?'

I fixed him with an intense stare as he answered.

'If he harms a hair on theirs or your head then I can promise you that he won't leave here alive.' Came the reply.

Chapter 83

As we moved along the dark hallway it became clear from the way that it flickered that the light in the window was coming from a single lit candle in the main living space. There were only two possible options on which way to go at the end of the short passageway, either through towards the candle or upstairs. Lee picked the downstairs since the light told us that somebody had been in there very recently, and I gestured that I was heading for the bedroom or rooms, I wasn't yet sure whether there was more than one up there. He looked deeply unhappy at the prospect of us parting ways and me being left alone, but he also knew that if we didn't split up then there was a much greater chance of him being able to slip away or creep up on us. After a moment's pause, in which we managed to have an entire conversation in silence communicating solely by exaggerated facial expressions, he accepted the situation for what it was and handed me the torch as he moved away towards the light.

I kept my feet at the furthest edges of the stair rungs, experience had taught me that they were less likely to squeak and groan there than in the middle where most people chose to tread and the wood began to flex and stretch. I could feel how cold it was up here as soon as my feet touched down on the tiny the landing, which made me shiver, but also gave me reassurance that I wasn't likely to open one of the two closed doors that had presented themselves to find the Grey Man inside wielding an axe. Odds were that there'd have been heat or light of some kind for him to keep warm or for him to work by. Easier to butcher bodies in the light than the dark.

I stopped at the first door and put my ear up against the wood before attempting to open it, I strained to listen, holding my breath to cut down on background noise but there were no obvious sounds coming from the other side. Gingerly I pushed down the handle, feeling and hearing the mechanism click softly and then toeing the door wide open and striking up a ridiculous approximation of a karate pose. As I suspected the room was devoid of life, and contained only a neat metal framed double bed, a large wooden wardrobe and mismatched chest of drawers.

I clicked on the small torch and swept the beam over chintzy floral soft furnishings and small stone sculptures. For a psycho he had surprisingly pleasant taste in décor.

I steadied myself and waited for my heart rate to come back down to a speed that didn't suggest I'd just run a marathon, taking a deep breath in, holding it for a couple of seconds and then letting it go. It was an old trick I'd been taught for bringing the body back out of a stress state more quickly. Realising that time was pressing on I forced myself to tackle the second door, once again putting my ear to the timber first. This time I could hear something inside, an odd gurgling sound like water or something thicker slowly draining away down a partially blocked sink. Every hair on the back of my neck stood up and my heartbeat went back into overdrive, while I involuntarily ran a dozen horrible images through my mind about what was inside making that sound. Whatever it was, I prayed it wasn't Lexie or Annabel, and that thought pushed aside my fear enough to drive me into action.

I stepped back away from the door and kicked out at the section just above and to the side of the handle with all of my force, feeling the surge of adrenaline as I connected and a section of the frame tore away, allowing the door to fly open unimpeded. I shone the meagre blue torchlight inside, realising immediately and with a vague spike of relief that it was a bathroom and that the noise could well have been just a blocked drain. That was when I saw the first of the blood, a handprint smear across one of the walls, more of it in spots and puddles on the lino floor and running down the tiles behind the sink. I heard the sound of Lee thundering back through the house and up the stairs to join me, startled by the crash as I'd smashed in the door, and I reached out and pulled the cord to switch on the main light. Then I saw

the woman in the bath, lying prone in an inch of her own blood with her face beaten beyond recognition. The low gurgling sound was coming from her.

Chapter 84

'Oh God. Is she...?'

Lee arrived on the scene two seconds after I'd switched the bathroom light on, taking in the horror scene that I was still trying to process for himself.

'No, she's making a noise that suggests she's still able to breathe, but it doesn't look good does it?'

He shook his head quickly in response as I looked around for something to stem her bleeding and settled on a couple of clean white bath towels.

'We're going to have to try to move her out of there so we can get a proper look at where all this blood's coming from besides her face.'

I moved around towards the lighter feet end and reached down into the tub and underneath the backs of her knees, immersing my hands and wrists in her cooling blood to achieve the feat. Lee wrapped his arms around her chest, tipping her forward so he could get around and under her arms, and getting a deep moan from her in response. That was a good sign. If she could still communicate her discomfort, and our backup arrived in record time, then she might just make it.

Thankfully she was only slightly built, because trying to manipulate a limp and badly injured person in the confined space of a bathroom, and without causing them further damage, is a recipe for disaster. The blood made her skin slippery to the touch, and more of it, both new and old, fell to the floor as we hauled her out onto one of the towels, trying hard to stay upright ourselves as the surface became a deadly skating rink.

'There are some deep cuts on her wrists and forearms, as well as a lot of blood from the facial damage, I say we do what we can for the arms and then finish off our search. I'm taking it you didn't find anything yet?'

I looked up at him and saw in his expression that there'd been nothing so far, before returning my attention to wrapping towels around the woman's wounds so he wouldn't see the pain in my expression. Judging by the grey hair and where we are, this has got to be Madeleine, the murderer's wife. So where are the girls and where is Reimoore?

'Nothing, but I was going to check out the garden when I heard all of the commotion. There's some kind of old shed down among the bushes, I think, and it looks like somebody had been digging some kind of pit or grave but got disturbed.'

He made the sudden connection between my question and its subtext, and realised what he'd just said.

'Oh shit. It could have been anything, and I got as far as having a quick look in before my attention was pulled this way. There was definitely nobody in it and I didn't see much blood anywhere downstairs.'

We moved the old lady onto her side and arranged her in the recovery position. Without a few years in medical school and some bags of plasma we couldn't do anything more for her at the moment anyway.

'Let's go check out that shed and the pit, and do me a favour and see where the hell armed response have got to. If he'd greeted us with a shotgun then we'd be two more to add to the tally by now.'

I couldn't keep the fear and anger out of my voice, there'd been a fuck up somewhere along the line and I couldn't decide whether that rested with me or elsewhere.

'Agreed.'

He stood up and caught a glimpse of his reflexion in the mirror behind my head, his hands and shirt were growing stiff with blood and gore, and a broad scarlet smear ran from the middle of his forehead down to the side of his right eyebrow where he'd touched his face with a bloody hand.

'Looking like we do at the moment, I'm betting we're odds on to end up face down on the ground with guns aimed at our heads when they do arrive.'

He offered a wry smile, since the comment was more observation than it was joke, and the 'gunslingers', as they were occasionally referred to, had a reputation for drawing their weapons at the slightest sign of trouble and asking questions later. Thankfully they weren't so quick to actually fire them.

Lee turned and stepped out of the door as I rose to follow close behind, and at that instant I heard an odd mechanical click and felt the air vibrate, just as he screamed and went down in a sudden hot spray of blood.

Chapter 85

He's been shot. I'm trapped in the bathroom with a dying woman and now the man I love is about to join her, and the Grey Man is out there with a gun waiting for me. The terror exploded inside me, wrapping a veil around my ability to reason and causing me to hyperventilate. Any moment I expected to see the barrel of a gun come into view around the doorframe, followed by his familiar face, and then that would be the end of my life. Long seconds stretched out, and finally I was able to rationalise again, realising that I'd heard a click and a vibration, not the deafening roar of a gun firing, and seeing Lee miraculously able to pull himself along the floor back into the bathroom.

'Shut the door too and we'll try to keep it pushed closed between us Za...'

He clenched his teeth against the pain and the colour started to drain out of his expression. It was almost impossible to see where he'd been hurt since he was already saturated in Madeleine's blood.

'What did he hit you with?'

I helped him the last couple of feet, taking hold of his arm and physically pulling him across the slick floor.

'A dart or an arrow of some kind...it passed straight through, I saw it embedded in the wall...I think he's hurt too...he was moving away from me as I fell, but his right arm was hanging down...'

His skin turned a horrible shade of grey and he vomited in his own lap. Not a gun, a crossbow, that's what the click was, and if he's wounded then he's going to have difficulty reloading it.

'Okay Lee, listen to me now, if you've got the strength then call in everything you can to the armed response team. When they finally choose to arrive I want them shooting at everything that moves that isn't us.'

I pressed the final semi-clean towel in the room into his hand so he could use it to stem his own bleeding and stood back up straight.

'What are you doing?'

He looked at me with wide imploring eyes, realising the answer to his own question and reaching out as if he intended to hang on to my trouser leg. I stepped away from reach and took hold of a heavy ceramic soap dish as the only likely makeshift weapon immediately to hand.

'I'm going after him. The girls could still be out in that shed or a room that hasn't been opened, and if they are they might still be alive. If I stayed in here while he went down there and butchered them then I couldn't live with the knowledge that I might have been able to stop him.'

He stretched out his arm again and I locked eyes with him so he could see that my mind was made up on this.

'Za...?'

His voice was weaker now as the pain really hit him hard.

'Yes?'

I crouched down to hear him properly.

'Don't get yourself killed or I'm going to have to join you.'

He smiled and I kissed him on top of the head.

'From where I'm standing you've got a head start at the moment. Now shut up and concentrate on stopping the rest of your blood from leaking out please. I'm not going to die today.'

I sounded much more certain than I felt as I stood back up and moved cautiously out through the broken door, scanning the shadows on the dark landing for signs of movement. He could be in the bedroom, there was time for him to hide in there while you were dithering and trying to find some courage. Your best course of action is to check there first and then go downstairs, but a bloody soap dish isn't going to help if he's headed for the knife drawer in the kitchen, even if he is injured.

I told myself off inside my head and realised that a better choice of weapon was staring me right in the face, the crossbow bolt that had passed through Lee and now jutted out of the landing wall. It was an effort to lever it back out, but the plaster work was old and beginning to lose its structure now, finally giving up the steel pointed dart and dislodging a shower of dust onto the floor. I held it like a miniature spear and set off to stalk and catch a killer.

Chapter 86

Nobody was waiting for me in the solitary bedroom and as I crept down the stairs, the rest of the house was quiet and watchful. The only original source of light, the candle that had been burning in the living room, had been snuffed out, although I couldn't say whether that was by accident or design, and the darkness was a heavy velvet cloak over everything. Halfway across the hallway I asked myself why I was still stalking along in the dark when I was already disadvantaged by surroundings that were entirely alien to me? Wherever he was lying in wait I wasn't realistically going to be aware of him before he was aware of me, so I might as well sacrifice the remote possibility of being so quiet that I somehow managed to sneak up on him, for the ability to see him coming when he made his presence known and came for me with murder in his eyes.

I flipped on the hall light and immediately felt better, illumination of any kind removes the biggest factor in fear every time - the unknown parts that your imagination fills in for you. This monster was terrifyingly real, I didn't need to let my mind embellish any of the details for me. Growing bolder I kicked the door off the hallway open and stepped back away, brandishing my crossbow bolt like a sword and then darting forwards to switch on the light in there too. Still no sign of the Grey Man, and I was starting to run out of lights and doors; he surely wasn't going to be afraid of me, so where the hell was he hiding?

Left with few other options, I moved through into the small

kitchen, starting to feel desperation setting in and kicking open the door to what I had thought was a pantry before I realised my error. What I saw inside made me felt momentarily queasy. There was a narrow long space with an assortment of jagged cutting tools, a large ceiling hook hanging over a gully that acted as a drain away, and worst of all a machine for mincing meat. At least I now knew where poor pretty Elizabeth Perry had met her end. I pulled the light on in there too, although there didn't seem to be anywhere to hide something the size of a full grown man, and saw dark stains showing through the glossy paint on the walls as I quickly switched it off again. I could detect the faint odour of raw meat coming from in the very fabric of the space, and I tried not to think about whether she, and others before her that had been in this room, had been alive or dead when he began to butcher them like slaughterhouse cattle.

Eventually I turned back away and closed the door again, overwhelmed with a sudden barrage of emotion at all of the suffering and all of the senseless loss of life because of the choices and actions of one damaged man. Okay lady, there'll be time to grieve for them later. Right now you need to get your act back together, or else you're going to be swinging from that hook yourself and watching your guts drop out onto the floor, followed pretty swiftly by Lee.

The only explanation left was that he'd headed out of the back door, which was bad news because we were out in woodland and I didn't exactly relish the prospect of trying to hunt him through bushes and around trees, without letting him get close enough to slit my throat. Would he have been able to reload his crossbow by now? I had no idea whether that feat could be accomplished with one hand, or without seeing his wounds for myself, if he was sufficiently mobile to be able to manage it with two hands anyway. He wouldn't have to sneak up on me then, he could just pick me off from a safe distance and then move in to finish the job when I was incapacitated.

A sound reached my ears from outside, a whoosh like petrol being ignited, which was so unexpected that I almost dismissed it as a product of my imagination, until I realised that an amber glow had filled the kitchen. It had to be him. I abandoned all caution and sprinted across the room, out of the door and straight into a nightmare.

Chapter 87

Tall flames were leaping up out of the pit in the middle of the garden, and the ferocious heat they were giving off forced me to put the brakes on my dash. Through the billowing clouds of black smoke I could see the figure of John Reimoore, the infamous killer who had labelled himself the Grey Man and who had confounded multiple police forces up and down the country, standing at the opposite side of the pit and staring straight at me. Just as Lee had said one of his arms hung uselessly down by his side, and he was spattered with blood, much of it seemingly from a wound that he'd taped up on his forehead. I thought back to the badly injured woman in the bath tub, his wife of so many years, and how I had entertained the suspicion that she was involved in his atrocious crimes. Now I was changing my mind.

He had both of the girls with him by the edge of the pit, wrists bound together with his signature knots no doubt, and Lexie was kneeling down in front of him while he held Annabel in a standing position with the blade of a large serrated hunting knife at her throat. Both of the girls were sobbing in abject terror, and blood and mud streaks were on their faces. The smoke and flames obscured some of my view, but I couldn't see any obvious injuries on them, so it seemed likely that the blood was not their own at least. I concealed the crossbow bolt next to my wrist in the hope that he had not seen it.

'I'm so pleased that you could join us, Zara. Do you know what it was going to be?'

He was forced to raise his voice to be heard over the crackle and roar of the flames, and he nodded towards the fiery pit and winced. The injury is to his shoulder and collarbone rather than the arm itself. I retained the information in case I could get close enough to him to put it to use.

'It looks like a primitive version of a barbecue, but on a larger scale.'

The words coming out of my mouth were calm and detached, completely at odds with how I felt, it was as if I was separating from my physical body and I wondered if I was already deep in shock.

'Not a bad guess.'

He smiled approvingly as if we were two old friends on an evening out and then carried on.

'Given sufficient time it would be a Fijian lovo. You don't usually cook with the flames, instead you let the fire die away, and there are particular types of stones in the base which retain heat for a very long time afterwards which you use to do the cooking. The meat is placed into the pit with the stones and then buried for several hours until it's so tender that it's practically falling of the bone, at which point you dig it up and feast. I've done it before when I was in the South Pacific, and it was delicious.'

He stopped to savour my reaction, but I was outwardly numb, existing somewhere deep inside myself that was designed to protect me from the reality of what was about to happen in front of my eyes. I saw the flash of annoyance on his face in the orange light, and felt

271

a fresh wave of searing heat as the breeze fanned the flames towards me.

'As much as it would be a waste, in the interests of time I may just have to use the flames after all on this occasion.'

He gestured as if to slash the standing girl's throat and pressed his knee to the back of Lexie as if to push her forwards into the fire, both of them closed their eyes as more tears squeezed out of the corners.

'NO, WAIT!'

I held up my hand and he stopped mid gesture looking amused.

'If you're going to try to appeal to my humanity then I can tell you now that you're wasting your time. I don't have any.'

The smile dropped away from him now, and I saw the sheen of madness in his eyes.

'Let them go and I will take their place in the flames, your letters were addressed to me, I'm the one that you want.'

I maintained eye contact and kept my voice calm and firm. inside I still felt strangely absent, but adrenaline began to drip slowly into my bloodstream in anticipation of what I was about to do. Reimoore relaxed his hold on Annabel and the knife moved precious inches away from her slim neck.

'Go on then. Throw yourself in.' He said, eyes narrowing in disbelief, and without hesitation I ran forward and leapt, knowing that I might not make the other side in one go, but needing to land close enough to continue the forward movement.

The heat of the fire blinded me as I passed through it and time seemed to slow to a near standstill, and then I was suddenly at the other side, screaming with my hair and clothes on fire as I thrust the crossbow bolt into the killer's chest and got my arm up between the knife and Annabel's throat.

Chapter 88

After an extended stay in hospital the world outside seemed to hold fresh new wonder, and I found myself transfixed by everything from morning dew on the petals of a rose, to the playful high jinks of a young boy with his Doberman puppy out on the park now. I'd taken to telling the kind faced psychologist from the occupational health unit that the nightmares had finally stopped, eager to get my mind back on work and away from the unwelcome flashbacks that haunt me. We both know that it's too soon for that to be true, but he is that rarity amongst the members of his profession from what I can see, and he has promised to sign me fit for office based duties at first. Followed by a gradual ease back into full duties later on, when my final skin graft operation is over and done with.

When the bad dreams do come they're mainly concerned with the final moments after I had leapt into the fire pit. The moments when I rolled around on the cool grass to put out my burning clothing and hair, hearing the death rattle of the Grey Man beside me over the screams and sobs of Lexie and Annabel, and I felt like my entire skin was melting away. Thankfully that hadn't been true, although the pain was excruciating, my burns were not at the worst end of the spectrum, and the majority of the damage had been done to my legs and the areas of my arms which were exposed by short sleeves. My face had been 'merely singed', to use the words of the cheerful nurses who had changed my dressings and administered more pain relief when the dull aching had grown back to an agonising roar. Now my hair was almost back to its unruly usual state, and I'd recovered the majority of my eyebrows, although the left one was noticeably more sparse than the right.

Lee's injury had been serious but not life-threatening in the end, the blood loss brought back under control when the troops had arrived to find the horror show that was waiting for them. Subsequent surgery had restored most of the mobility to his shoulder joint, although it was never going to be quite the way it had been before. Bless him, but he was deeply ashamed that he'd not been able to come to my rescue in what he saw as my hour of need, and I'd had to have stern words with him in order to partially snap him back out of it.

Unfortunately the woman in the bathroom, who had indeed been Madeleine as we'd suspected, had not been so lucky. She'd held on for long enough to make it to the hospital, which was nothing short of miraculous in view of the amount of blood that she'd lost, but then died on the operating table as surgeons tried to do something about the catastrophic brain injuries that had been sustained.

Lexie and Annabel were staying with mine and Emily's parents now, Emily had been released from hospital and predictably gone back to David again now, but was not deemed to be in a position to cater for their additional needs yet. Outwardly at least, we were all hopeful that the situation would change soon. My heart bled for both of the girls, and all that they'd had to see and endure. I'd wanted to pull them into my arms and tell them that everything was okay now when I'd killed Reimoore right in front of them, but I was in too much pain to speak or to be touched, and they'd been forced to sit beside me until our backup had arrived, not knowing whether I would live or die too. So much pain and horror at such a young age and from the ones that they'd been taught to love and trust the most. It was going to take time, patience and luck for their scars to fully heal. I'd been told to expect that mine never would, although their appearance would improve eventually.

A serial murder case doesn't end for those involved with the apprehension or death of the offender, since there are still so many evidential loose ends to tie up and other potential victims to identify in order to give surviving friends and relatives their imperfect closure. However, I knew from the updates that Geeta Badal and Lee had been relaying to me in hospital that those lines of enquiry were in capable hands, and that we were getting that much closer each day to putting the final pieces of the puzzle together. I looked forward to pitching in too, when circumstances would allow, but first I'd have to go through the remaining absurd formalities to clear my own name of wrongdoing in respect of the death of John Reimoore by my hand.

Chapter 89

Lee had continued to stay at my place while I had been lying in a hospital bed, and it looked like he'd be a permanent fixture for the foreseeable future too. He'd initially promised during one of our long visits to stop trying to find a new place until I was back up and running again, but over the last few weeks the conversation had tentatively moved towards the possibility of us pooling our collective resources and finding something new and bigger for both of us to live in on a permanent basis. The prospect was exciting but also a little scary, so our compromise had been to spend six months checking that we didn't drive each other crazy before we took the leap.

It felt strange walking back up my own driveway again, but comforting to be back in control of my own schedule. I've never been a very good patient. Once I was inside I saw that Lee had neatly stacked up my mail on the dining table and thoroughly spring cleaned the whole place, and I smiled at a note that he'd left with 'tonight's menu' scrawled onto it. Moving through the lounge I also noticed that all signs of the orange stains from Emily's spaghetti throwing escapade were gone, God only knew how, but the carpet and upholstery was pristine, and I felt the prickling of joyful tears coming on.

'Detective Sergeant Lee Mead, I love you very much indeed.'

I announced to the empty space, lifting up the first bundle of mail and sifting through for signs of anything interesting.

I made my way into the kitchen for coffee and a mooch around the fridge, recognising some of the envelopes as bills and others as junk, and depositing the junk ones directly in the bin. Several more were unfamiliar, and I opened them to find that not only had I apparently won a large cash prize in a competition that I'd never entered, but I was also due compensation for an accident that I had no recollection of having been involved in too. Both of those swiftly joined their friends in the recycling bin as well.

I discarded what was left of the pile on the worktop and sorted out a mug of coffee, making it strong and sweet and settling on a biscuit after an appraisal of the fridges contents turned up nothing of interest that would serve as a snack. A sudden unexpected clattering of the letterbox made me jump and spill some of my coffee on the floor, and I swore loudly, throwing a cloth down and using my foot to mop up the worst of the mess. The post gets later and later these days, it used to come first thing in the morning. I was flustered and embarrassed by my reaction, not wanting the unwelcome reminder that I wasn't quite in the rude health that I wanted to kid myself I was.

I pulled myself back together quickly, discarding the cloth in the sink and trotting briskly back through into the hallway to retrieve the mail. Only one letter awaited me, lying face down on the mat, and I stooped to pick it up, turning it over in my hands. As soon as I saw the writing on the front I dropped it back to the floor again as if it was tainted, feeling the tension returning to my body and finding it hard to catch my breath. The handwriting was the Grey Man's scrawl, I recognised it from all of the other scenes. Hundreds of times I'd run through the contents, so often that I knew I couldn't be mistaken. I rushed to the window to try to catch sight of who had delivered it, but was greeted with the sight of a leather clad figure on a motorbike roaring away into the distance.

Trembling, I forced myself to lift it for a second time and tore open the envelope, taking the letter to the dining table and sitting down to read.

What is the colour of pain? Sometimes I've convinced myself that it's the red of spilling blood, or the purple and pink of viscera, but then I change my mind and I settle on the absence of colour that is black again – the void into which we all must pass one day.

My father taught me important lessons and gave me his name, as his father had done for him in turn before that, the chain stretching both back into the past and onwards into the future, and in doing so he secured a legacy.
You won't appreciate the sentiment, given to imperfect thoughts. But some of us are born special, with special minds that give us the permission to take the lives of others, if it pleases us to do so – hunters one and all – everybody else is prey.

As I write this I have the feeling that someday we'll meet again, in this life or the next. My legacy will outlive me and perhaps revisit you someday if I cannot.

279

Grey Man

Chapter 90

It was three in the afternoon on a Wednesday, and after numerous calls, messages left and a lot of very much against the grain pleading, Emily was finally sitting opposite me in a coffee shop in Leamington Spa. She kept her over-sized dark glasses on indoors and had not returned my smile of greeting when I'd arrived, but at least she was here, which gave me the chance to say what I needed to say to her.

'You've lost weight again, sis, there's practically nothing left of you now!'

I tried to break the ice gently as a waitress took our order of two skinny latte's and scurried away to fetch them.

'I've not had much appetite recently, and neither has David after everything that's happened.'

Her reply was a flat monotone, nothing moving on her face except her mouth, and I wondered whether she was heavily medicated at the moment and if that was why the glasses had stayed in place. This time I damned well wasn't going to pry though.

'I can imagine. I've not been feeling on top of the world myself. How has he been?'

I tried to remain impassive while I looked for an opening to get through to her without tipping her over the edge again.

'What do you care? You hate him, he told me about how you got your boyfriend to beat him up when he came round looking for me, and don't deny it, I saw the bruises at the time when he came to see me in hospital, right around the time you stopped bothering to visit.'

An unmistakeable trace of bitterness crept into her delivery this time, and I saw how cleverly he'd been manipulating the situation.

'Just so you've got your facts straight, Lee only hit him after he'd assaulted me and forced his way into my house. If I was malicious then I could have had him locked up for either of those things, but I didn't do so, and I was told by the hospital staff that you had specifically asked them to stop me from visiting you. No prizes for guessing who really engineered that situation now are there?'

I quickly reached out across the table and pulled her sunglasses off her face, expecting to see glazed eyes but seeing livid purple and green bruising instead.

'Give them back NOW!'

The sentence started out as a hiss and ended in a shout as I gave them back to her, and the other occupants of the café turned to stare at us. Emily angrily arranged the glasses back over her face and immediately stood up to leave, grabbing her handbag off the table. The poor waitress arrived with our drinks at that moment and froze in place, not sure whether to put them down or not.

'It's okay, just drop them on the table for us please.' I said and offered a strained smile as I set off in pursuit of Emily.

'I suppose those bruises are my fault too, on account of how I killed his psychopath father. Is that what he tells you?'

I grabbed her arm and saw her look down at the scarring where my sleeve had ridden up.

'Emily, there's a good chance that David's guilty of worse than being an abusive husband, and I need you to listen to me on this, even if you still decide not to have anything else to do with me afterwards.'

She stopped trying to pull away now, and I saw a tear on her cheek creeping out from under the bottom of the shades.

'I received a final letter from John Reimoore a few days ago, which somebody posted on his behalf after his death, and I think that same person is the one who threw a severed head at me outside Lee's house before that. I can't prove it yet, but I believe that at the very least David's been involved in helping his father in the commission of some of these recent offences.'

I let go of her arm and cupped her head in my hands.

'If I'm right then he's crazy, and a significant danger to you too, and I need you to help me by removing yourself from harm's way. Remember what you told me about what you felt he was capable of before?'

A long moment passed in which she stared blankly at me, and then she reached up and pulled my hands away, pressing them firmly back against my own chest.

'You're the one who's crazy. David is not a monster just because he was fathered by one, and I want you to stay the hell away from us.'

She said, turning her back on me and walking out of the doors and slowly up the street. I watched as she stopped beside a leather-clad figure on a motorbike and put on a helmet of her own, climbing on behind them and holding around the drivers waist without looking back. The figure in leathers raised an open hand towards me in mock greeting, and waved once before setting off, leaving me stood powerless to stop them with the words of a dead killer replaying in my mind.

What is the colour of pain? I settled on the absence of colour that is black again – the void into which we all must pass one day. My legacy will outlive me and perhaps revisit you someday if I cannot.

3159476R00151

Printed in Great Britain
by Amazon.co.uk, Ltd.,
Marston Gate.